WE[...]

In spring, the r[...] by trees of pale-g[...], it becomes a lea[...] sun splashes, winding its way towards the village. Along the coast, overhanging trees tilt above the sea and ancient roots swirl in the incoming tide. These tangled woodlands are all that is left of a vast forest land that was once called Trá na Coille.

In those far-off days, it was a wild, lonely place. Families fished along its coast. Farmers cleared the land and built their settlements from the strong oak wood. In medieval times, King Henry II granted the forests and a royal title to an officer from Bristol, James Hobourne. A castle was built and trees were felled to create a rich, pastoral estate for Lord and Lady Hobourne.

As the centuries passed, Trá na Coille became Beachwood. The trees continued to be felled, their strong timbers furnishing fine houses and mighty warships. Its population farmed and fished and traded, or they worked on the Hobourne estate which was located to the north of Dublin city. In 1970, the Hobourne family sold their lands and home to the Irish Government. Hobourne House became the local secondary school. Land was sold for development and housing estates were built with names like Oaktree, Cypress, Elmgrove and Ashwood. The gardens and grounds were turned into a public park. The population grew, and in Hobourne Park, young people began to gather in Fountain Square.

Today it is their favourite meeting spot. Ask them about Beachwood and they will tell you that it is a magic place with the sea and the city and the country all rolled up together. But during the winter months, when the trees form a bleak guard-of-honour and the grey sea lashes the coast, they will complain that it is Drearsville, on the edge of nowhere. I would like to introduce you to these young people as they move through the seasons. Join them on their good days and their bad days. Dance and play, fight, grieve, love and laugh with them. But most of all, enjoy them.

SCHOOL BULLY

BEACHWOOD

SCHOOL BULLY

JUNE CONSIDINE

POOLBEG

First published 1993 by
Poolbeg Press Ltd
Knocksedan House,
Swords, Co Dublin, Ireland

© June Considine 1993

The moral right of the author has been asserted.

A catalogue record for this book is available from the British Library.

ISBN 1 85371 260 4

All rights reserved. No part of this publication may be reproduced or transmitted in any form or by any means, electronic or mechanical, including photography, recording, or any information storage or retrieval system, without permission in writing from the publisher. The book is sold subject to the condition that it shall not, by way of trade or otherwise, be lent, resold or otherwise circulated without the publisher's prior consent in any form of binding or cover other than that in which it is published and without a similar condition including this condition being imposed on the subsequent purchaser.

Cover design by Pomphrey Associates
Cover illustration by Brian Caffrey
Set by Mac Book Limited in Stone 9.5/13
Printed by Cox & Wyman,
Reading, Berks

Cast of Characters

Young People

Tom Parkinson

Jennifer Hilliard

Caro Kane, Jennifer's friend

Danny Kane, Caro's elder brother

Keith Fowler (Freaky)

Liam Egan (Ugly)

Duane Ryder

Oliver Kerr

Michael and David Hilliard, Jennifer's twin brothers

Lorraine Crowe

Andrew Lee

Red Prescott

Liz O'Rourke

Aoife Johnston ⎱ Friends of Jennifer and Caro
Emma Patton ⎰

(all except Danny Kane are classmates of Tom Parkinson)

Teachers

Mrs Belton, Form teacher and English teacher

Mr Brown, Geography

Mrs McColl, Science

Mr Twomey, Maths

Adults

Helen Parkinson, Tom's mother

Conor O'Carroll, Helen's friend

Thomas O'Meara, Tom's father, an Australian

Jenny Burrows, "The Sex Woman"

Mrs Maxwel, Thomas O'Meara's grandmother

Dr Darcy

Mrs Fowler, local busybody

Mrs Kane, mother of Caro and Danny

Locations

Mill Hill, Tom's home

Elmtree Close

The Greasy Spoon

Limestone House

Beachwood Comprehensive

Fountain Square

Twist and Shake

Railway Embankment

Ternville House

To my nephew Stephen Mullally

Prologue

Helen Parkinson was seventeen years old when she met Thomas O'Meara. He sounded far too Irish to be an Australian but Melbourne was where he had spent the first eighteen years of his life. He was a tall, rangy young man with dark-brown eyes, big feet and a way of making everyone who stood near him look small. Helen lived in Mill Hill on the outskirts of Beachwood with her father, who was the local solicitor. She was a soft-spoken and studious girl, who was determined to go to university when she finished secondary school. She was small, not even reaching Thomas's shoulder, and her auburn hair, split in the centre, framed a heart-shaped face. It was Conor O'Carroll, her friend and neighbour, who introduced them to each other.

Conor lived in an old house with a muddy driveway and a sprawl of stables at the back. His mother gave riding lessons to the local children and Conor helped out in the stables in his spare time. Thomas, as horse-obsessed as Conor, was in the stables when Helen arrived one day.

"Boy meets girl. Wham!" Conor said to himself and watched them fall in love in front of his eyes. All the boys Helen Parkinson had ever thought she fancied, all the love-games she had ever played became a sport for children compared to this new, wonderful sensation. Her feelings were returned in full by the young man with the twanging accent and a six-week holiday that seemed to stretch endlessly before them.

Thomas was on a visit to Beachwood with his Irish-born parents. His family had spent one month in Cork with his father's family and had arrived in the small coastal village in Dublin to stay for six weeks with his widowed grandmother, Mrs Maxwell.

The young couple met every day. They kissed in Magpie Cave and behind the sand dunes. They walked for miles along the estuary path, arms around each other, footsteps moving together in a slow, dreamy rhythm. Six weeks seemed forever and when it was over, it ended with such devastating suddenness that neither could understand where their time had gone.

For six weeks Helen had been able to forget. Her mother had died the previous year and her father had hardly spoken to her since that day. He had been middle-aged when she was born and was a strict father, loving his only daughter in a formal, silent way. Mr Parkinson disapproved of young people. He disliked their morals, their clothes and their hairstyles. He believed that they showed no respect for their elders and their music drove him into a frenzy. Mrs Parkinson winked at Helen when her husband ranted on about such things. As soft-spoken as her daughter, she was a cushion for Helen against the demands of her father. She allowed Helen's friends into the house when he was at work and cheerfully turned a deaf ear to the record player when it blasted out the latest hit songs. When she died, after a short and hopeless fight against cancer, Mr Parkinson suffered his grief in silence. His face closed over and his lips clenched when Helen tried to console him. Like two strangers, father and daughter lived together. She cooked their meals and kept the house tidy.

He handed over money for bills and food. Slowly, painfully, a new order was restored to their lives.

For Helen, meeting Thomas O'Meara was like walking into sunshine after being imprisoned in a dank, grey mist. The thought of returning to the mist made her cry bitterly in the dark shelter of the sand dunes on Thomas's last night before returning to Australia.

Her father believed that she was going into Dublin city to the cinema with a girl friend. He had ordered her to be home by ten o'clock. But the hour had slipped by and the balmy August night was stealing their time away. They promised to write to each other. They promised to think about each other at a certain time each day and their thoughts would unite them for that instant. But Helen began to cry because it was so difficult to work out the time differences between Ireland and Australia. It was very important that neither would be asleep at that special moment.

But the tears were not just over Thomas's departure. Her mother had also left her and her father's silent rejection was a wound that time was not healing. All these thoughts came together and then he was holding her close, so close, and for the first time, she did not care about what tomorrow would bring. When they left the sand dunes, the new moon was a pale, silver shadow in the black sky.

Her father was waiting for her, demanding to know where she had been, refusing to believe her stammered excuses about missing her bus and having to wait an hour for the next one. In the end he gave a resigned sigh and told her that she was grounded for the next three weeks.

Helen nodded. It was a matter of complete indifference to her. For once she was glad that he was so wrapped up in his own misery and did not notice her guilty, tear-stricken face. She saw the plane flying overhead next morning. It seemed to dip over Beachwood Strand and the sun glinted fiercely on the wings.

When school term started, she returned to Beachwood

Comprehensive and tried to concentrate on studying for her Leaving Certificate examination. This was her important year. It would determine her future and whether or not she would go to university.

For two months she refused to believe it. Her mind shied away from the thought and her heart beat so frantically with panic that she was sure the other students sitting next to her would hear it. She received three letters from Thomas but was unable to reply to any of them. How could she when there was only one thing she could tell him? There was nothing to say until she could admit the dawning truth to herself.

"Is something wrong, Helen?" Mrs Belton, her English teacher, stopped her in the corridor one day. The teacher's expression was shrewd as she looked at Helen's thin, pale face and haunted eyes.

"No! Why should anything be wrong?" Helen replied and began to sob at the sheer terror of it all.

Mrs Belton gently prised the story from her. A visit to Dr Darcy confirmed the fears that had tormented Helen since the night she had said goodbye to Thomas in the dunes of Beachwood Strand.

On Mill Hill, Helen's father stared in horror at her. "Pregnant. My only daughter...pregnant!"

Soon, the rumour mill at Beachwood Comprehensive was humming. A teenage pregnancy was big news. Helen's friends were sympathetic but when she walked through Beachwood Village, she was conscious of eyes watching her. She felt as if she was living in a goldfish bowl, able to see but not to hear what was being said outside her glass shield.

Her father brought her to Elmtree Close to talk the matter over with Thomas's grandmother. Mrs Maxwell had iron-grey hair and faded, bird-like eyes that turned chilly when Mr Parkinson told her the reason for his visit. She tightened her lips and said that Thomas was a respectable lad and that he would never dream of doing such a thing. Mr Parkinson ignored her outburst and said she must contact her grandson immediately. Thomas O'Meara must return to Beachwood and accept his responsibility.

"You want him to travel from Australia, give up his place in university, get married at eighteen because your daughter tells you she's expecting his baby? I'll do no such thing!" replied Mrs Maxwell. "What proof have you got that it's Thomas's baby, that's what I want to know?"

Mr Parkinson was furious. A vein throbbed in his forehead. He looked like an old, bewildered man and when he met Helen's eyes she saw the shame she had brought on him reflected in his gaze.

That night Helen wrote to Thomas and told him everything. For six weeks she waited for a reply. She would wake early each morning, her ears strained for the sound of a letter falling through the letterbox. She waited for the phone to ring.

Whenever a plane flew over Beachwood Strand, she wondered if he was on it, hurrying towards her to make everything all right again. Her father also contacted the O'Meara family in Australia. Mrs O'Meara refused to believe such a vile story. Her son had denied being the father of Helen's baby. As far as Mrs O'Meara was concerned, that was the end of the matter.

Mr Parkinson made arrangements for his daughter to travel to England and stay with her Aunt Maria, who lived in a quiet London suburb. When the baby was born, it would be adopted immediately. He refused to discuss

Helen's wishes, to listen to her pleas that she be allowed to keep her baby.

"Will you at least come over to me when it's time for the birth?" she asked him on the night before her departure.

"Your aunt will be able to manage that sort of thing better than I could," he replied and buried himself behind his daily copy of *The Irish Times*.

In that instant, Helen felt herself moving away from her father. Not in a physical sense because she was able to kiss him good night and hug him hard for the last time. But in her mind, there was a deep sea between them which neither would ever be able to cross. She walked along Beachwood Strand the following morning. A cold November wind blew harshly through the sand dunes. Conor O'Carroll was riding a horse at the edge of the sea shore. He reined in and dismounted when he saw her.

"I can't understand it. Thomas was nuts about you." He ran his hand distractedly through his red hair. "Why didn't he reply? I even wrote to him myself. If it was me...!"

She put her fingers over his lips. "Shush. It's over. I'll be all right. Have you got the address?"

He pulled a piece of paper from the pocket of his jeans and handed it to her. "I wish there was something more I could do."

"Just keep it a secret, please. Don't tell my father where I am. That's all I ask."

"You know I won't." He hugged her. "You must keep in touch with me. Let me know how you get on."

At Heathrow Airport, she lingered by the luggage conveyor belt until all the passengers had entered the arrivals area. When she finally emerged, her aunt was nowhere to be seen. A message was being relayed over the loudspeaker, asking Helen Parkinson to report to an information desk. The airport was bustling with passengers, a busy anonymous place. Helen quickly made her way to the underground station. Soon she was hurtling in a tube towards the centre of London. She emerged into daylight and watched the colourful population of London hurrying past. Everyone seemed to move on skates, to have their faces pressed towards some distant place which they hoped to reach as quickly as possible. They did not notice the small girl with the long auburn hair hiding her face. After living for four months with the eyes of Beachwood skimming over her still-slim waistline, the joy of being part of a crowd was wonderful.

Conor had given her an address in Camden Town and she eventually reached Ternville House, an old, three-storey building with peeling paint on the outside and a group of young, Irish people living inside. They were Conor's friends and had been expecting her.

It was an untidy, noisy house with a moving population that came and went at all times of day or night and never needed an excuse to throw a party.

When Helen's son was born she named him Thomas. The wild, young men and women in Ternville House immediately called him Tom Thumb and held a celebration party that lasted for two days. Even when old Mrs Thompson, who owned the house and lived in two rooms upstairs, complained about the noise, they brought her down and taught her how to play the bodhrán.

For a year, Helen lived rent free in Ternville House, cooking and caring for everyone and trying to bring some order to their lives. It was an exhausting time filled with quiet moments when the house was empty and she could sit with her baby in her arms. There was never any shortage of willing babysitters. They wheeled Tom around the Camden markets and to the top of Primrose Hill where they sang songs to him and carried him piggyback to the bottom. At night they put him to bed while Helen attended night college and did a secretarial skills course.

On the day of her arrival in London, Helen had sent a postcard, with no address, to her father to tell him she was safe. He did not hear from her again until Tom's first birthday. This time she included her address and invited him to come to London and meet his grandson. She enclosed a photograph that Barry, one of the young men in the house, had taken. Her father sent back Tom's photograph and the letter, unread.

Years passed. The young people left Ternville House. Some married, some returned to Ireland, others emigrated further afield.

Barry went to the Malaysian Rain Forests to photograph plants and trees that could soon become extinct due to the cutting down of the trees.

Ternville House grew quiet. Ambitious, hard-working yuppy couples rented the rooms and were too busy making money to have time for parties. Old Mrs Thompson sighed because there was nothing to complain about except the loudness of Tom's radio. Helen rented three rooms. She worked as a secretary for an electronics company called Techlore Trading. Her long auburn hair was neatly cut. Her jeans were replaced by neat skirts and blouses with lace collars. She was the perfect secretary.

Still she heard no word from her father. She told herself that she did not care. Her home was in Ternville House and the life she had known in the sleepy village of

Beachwood belonged to a young girl who no longer existed.

Chapter One

1 *1.30 p.m. My grandfather died today on Beachwood Golf Course at 6pm precisely, just as he had finished playing the eighteenth hole. He pitched forward and was dead by the time he hit the green. Full blast-off to heaven. A man called Conor O'Carroll rang us with the news. He is taking care of things until we arrive in Ireland. I never met my grandfather. But, tomorrow I will, when we fly over for his funeral. My mother's nervous. She can't stop talking when she's like that and since she heard the news she's been blowing my ear off. She never said much about my grandfather when he was alive but she told me loads about him tonight. I'm not surprised she ran away from him when she was seventeen. It will be her first time back in Beachwood since then. I wonder what a corpse looks like? Lester said his grandfather was stone cold—and yellow like frozen butter.*

I'm frightened.

On a crisp Friday morning in January, Tom Parkinson looked out of the plane window and saw a white fringe of foam lapping against the Irish coastline. He looked quickly away from the dizzying drop below him. He hated heights, dreaded them, fought with them and was defeated by them. His mother held tightly to his sweating hand. Helen Parkinson looked far too young to be the mother of a thirteen-and-a-half-year-old son. All his friends said she was more like his older sister. "It will be over in a minute, Tom. Just hold on. You'll be all right."

Last night, it was he who had held her hand after the phone call, when the streaky tears kept running down her cheeks.

"I wonder did he think of me, Tom?" she said. "Just before he died, did he wonder what his life would have been like if he'd known you?"

The plane screeched along the runway until it seemed that a giant hand had gripped its tail and pulled it to an instant, shuddering stop. They collected their luggage and walked out into the arrivals lounge of Dublin Airport.

"Helen Parkinson. You darling girl! Come here and give me a hug!" shouted a tall, red-haired man. He swept Tom's mother into his arms.

"Conor O'Carroll! You haven't changed a bit!" Helen began to weep into his shoulder, then hugged him back with the same fierce enthusiasm.

Within a few minutes, they were being driven in Conor's car along a busy dual carriageway. Gradually the road narrowed and began to wind around sharp bends where high, leaning trees threw shadows before them. From the back seat, Tom watched Conor O'Carroll's eyes. They were a startlingly bright-blue shade and one of them winked back at him. A bus came towards them with a sign on the front that read *Trá na Coille* and, underneath, the word *Beachwood*.

"Trá na Coille." His mother seemed to breathe the words. "That's the Irish name for Beachwood, Tom." It was the first time he had ever heard her use the language. It sounded strange and soft on her tongue.

The main street of Beachwood Village was heavy with traffic. Helen peered intently from the passenger seat window. "Beachwood seems to have changed a lot, Conor. It's more...modern. Busier. I don't remember that shopping centre. Or those townhouses."

"Fourteen years is a long time, Helen. There are bound to be changes."

The funeral home had stained-glass windows and soft carpets that muffled Tom's footsteps. His mother linked his arm, tightly. When she stood over her father's coffin, she gave a great gasp as if she were choking. His grandfather was a thin, waxy statue, a yellow-grey colour with closed eyes and his hands crossed on his chest. Tom looked down at him and could think of nothing to say. He did not want to touch him. Even when the men in black coats and solemn faces put the lid on the coffin and his grandfather's body was driven to a small church with a high spire, he could still not feel any emotion other than curiosity about this stern-faced man who had driven his daughter from his house fourteen years earlier and had never forgiven her for giving birth to Tom.

After the removal service, a line of people walked up the aisle of the church to shake Helen's hand. Some hugged her warmly, particularly a woman called Stella Kane. By her side stood a girl about Tom's own age with black bobbed hair and thick dark eyebrows.

"So, you're Tom!" Mrs Kane pressed his hands between

her own. "You must come and meet my gang before you return to London. This one's called Caroline but there are three more. You *will* bring him, Helen?"

Helen smiled and nodded before turning to greet the person standing behind Mrs Kane. The black-haired girl grinned at Tom and then sobered instantly as if unsure whether one was allowed to grin at a removal service.

That night, Tom stayed in a hotel called the Swansbury. It had bay windows overlooking Swansbury Estuary and he sat in a deep armchair opposite his mother. They watched the moon's reflection on the water. A lone heron stood on one leg and seemed to stare intently back at them. Young couples walked along the estuary path, holding hands, heads close together. A half-smile played over Helen Parkinson's lips.

"What are you thinking about?" Tom asked.

"Ghosts," she replied, softly. "Go to bed, Tom. Tomorrow will be a long day."

After the funeral, Tom was amazed at the way everyone stood around the grave with its pyramid of freshly-cut flowers. In London, the only funeral he had attended had been the cremation of Lester's grandfather. After the service ended, the mourners had shaken hands politely with Lester's family and driven away. But in this Irish graveyard, people talked in loud voices and even laughed. One old man boasted to Tom that he was ninety-five years old and looked extremely pleased that it was William Parkinson, Solicitor, and not himself who was lying under the artificial bright-green carpet of grass. The girl with the dark eyebrows smiled at Tom. He tried to remember her name but his mind had been a blur since his arrival in Ireland.

"I'm Caro," she said. "We met yesterday. What do you

think of Beachwood? Isn't it a real dump?" Her voice was fondly possessive and she would have been furious if he dared agree with her.

"It looks nice," replied Tom. "But I've seen very little of it."

"I'll show you around. You're coming over to our place tomorrow for Sunday lunch. I think your accent's cute." Caro grinned. "Real Prince Charles stuff."

"Steady on!" He was horrified. Traces of his mother's Irish accent were mixed with his own and in London his friends said that he sounded like Bob Geldof, which was almost as bad.

"There's an angel over there that looks the image of Princess Di. Would you like to see it?" Because he was from London, Caro seemed to believe that he had an abiding interest in such things. He wanted to tell her that he was an anti-royalist and had no interest in any member of the royal family. But he was anxious to escape from the strangers who kept hugging him, shaking his hand and staring at him with great curiosity. He followed her as she hopped carefully over a grave. They stopped in front of the statue of a dramatic-looking angel with huge marble wings. He didn't think the angel looked at all like Princess Di, except for a demure sideways gaze. Two women were talking intently to each other and did not notice them.

"I wonder what poor Mr Parkinson would say if he knew his grandson was attending his funeral?" The woman who spoke had a round, pasty face. She wore bright-red lipstick and when her lips puckered with disapproval, they reminded Tom of smeared jam on a doughnut.

"He might be glad," said her companion. "He should

have made peace with his daughter years ago. By the time a funeral comes, it's too late to settle family quarrels."

"She was to blame!" said the woman with the doughnut face. She had a bossy voice, loud and carrying. "As for that boy. Now that I've seen him, there's no mystery about his father. He's the spitting image of that Australian lad she used to hang around with."

Caro began to cough, spluttering and clearing her throat in an exaggerated way. When the women noticed Tom, there was an abrupt silence. Quickly, they hurried away from the shelter of the angel's wings.

"Are you all right, Tom?" Caro was looking anxiously at him.

"Yes," he replied, stiffly. "Who's that woman with the lipstick?"

Her nose wrinkled. "Mrs Fowler. She's an awful gossip. Yap! Yap! Yap! Don't mind anything she says."

"She has a face like a doughnut!"

"You're right!" Caro shrieked, then clapped her hand to her mouth. "I keep forgetting where I am."

"I'm sure my grandfather wouldn't mind."

"Oh he would. He was a real grump. If we called to him with sponsorship cards, he used to shake his walking stick at us. Do you mind me saying that?"

"Not in the least," replied Tom, politely.

Back at the Swansbury Hotel, he remembered Mrs Fowler's words. No one had ever told him that he looked like his father. He stared at his reflection in the mirror and saw a long thin face with wide-spaced brown eyes and dark-brown hair swept to one side. He tried to imagine an older face, lines around the eyes, stubble on the chin, a few grey hairs among the brown. An impossible image.

Next day Caro introduced him to her friend, Jennifer Hilliard. "Be nice to her," she warned. "Her father's the local sergeant and he'll put you in jail if you're not."

Jennifer grinned ruefully, obviously well used to being teased about her father. She was a tall, noisy girl with shoulder-length blonde hair and a ringing laugh. Tom thought she was the most gorgeous girl he had ever met. The three of them walked down to Beachwood Village. Helen had given them money and the girls brought him to the sweetshop, Sherbet Alley, where Caro's older sister, Susan, worked at the weekends. A group of boys hung around outside a fast food takeaway called The Greasy Spoon. They whistled at the girls and deliberately blocked Tom's path so that he was forced off the pavement. In the evening, Tom went with the girls to a film in a cinema complex nicknamed the WUC. The same group of boys sat in front of them. They kept tossing popcorn back at the girls. One of them leaned around and tried to put his hand on Jennifer's leg.

"Get knotted, Keith Fowler!" she bellowed and swatted him away like a fly. Immediately a cinema usher with a torch waved it in their direction.

"What's going on here?" he demanded, aiming his torch suspiciously at them. Everyone stared intently at the screen. "Any more messing and you're all out on your ear," he warned, before moving on.

"You met the mother," said Caro, nudging him and lowering her voice. "Now meet the son. Freaky Fowler. He's such a bully but he thinks he's so cool. Those airheads who hang around him can't take a deep breath without asking his permission."

On the day of their departure for London, Tom went with his mother and Conor O'Carroll to see the house on

Mill Hill where Helen had lived until she was seventeen. It looked like a mansion compared to their flat in Ternville House. On the driveway, gravel crunched beneath their feet. Helen hesitated at the entrance to the house and Conor put his arm around her waist to guide her through the doorway. The furniture was old-fashioned, shabby armchairs with faded, flowery covers, a dark-wood piano with photographs on the top. Helen lifted up a photograph of her mother. "Meet your grandmother, Tom. She would have loved you."

Since the night of the phone call, she had been weeping and laughing in equal measure. Tom waited until she wiped her eyes and blew her nose before replacing the photograph. "She looks just like you," he said. "I'd have loved her too." He examined photographs of Helen as a young girl. The discovery that his mother had once had a life without him had been a strange experience. Before his birth she had cut all her links with that world and it had never been part of his upbringing. But, in Beachwood, he kept meeting strangers who greeted her in a familiar manner and spoke about places, people and things of which he had no knowledge. Even his mother, with her sudden mood swings, seemed different, as if, in the cold, musty atmosphere of her father's house, her past was crowding around her.

"Are you sure you won't change your mind?" Conor was asking her a question. "I know your father would have wanted you to live here. With the sale of his business, you wouldn't have to worry about money."

Leave London? Impossible! Tom stood still, hardly daring to breathe until his mother shook her head.

"If that was what he wanted, then why didn't he get in touch with me. I gave him enough opportunities. It's too late now. The house is to be sold as soon as possible, Conor. Will you take care of it for me?" Her tone was harsh and final. The red-haired man sighed but he did not seem surprised by her refusal.

Upstairs, from the back bedroom window, they looked out over the long, overgrown garden which was fenced off by a wall. Beyond the wall, there was a narrow path that fell away into a steep embankment of grass and rock, leading down towards a railway track. It made Tom dizzy just to look at it.

"This was my room, Tom," said Helen. "I used to hear the trains going past and I'd know what time it was without having to look at my watch."

"It was the same with me." Conor pointed towards a cluster of trees between the houses. "You can't see my place from here but it's just beyond those trees. It also backs on to the embankment. I once tried to climb down to the tracks for a dare and was so terrified half-way down that I had to be rescued and brought to the top. Talk about losing face! The only person I ever knew who made that climb was...was...Thomas."

"I remember that day. I was so frightened that he'd fall." Helen kept staring at the distant tracks, her face averted from them.

Tom wandered down the stairs and out into the back garden. It was long and tangled with weeds. Nettles stung his hand and his trousers snagged on hidden brambles. He heard laughter and a scuffling sound from inside a wooden shed close to the garden wall. He opened the door. Four boys sat on wooden boxes. They were smoking cigarettes and playing cards. Tom recognised Keith Fowler and the boys from the cinema. They were just as startled by his appearance. It was obvious that they used the shed regularly as a den. Crisp bags, mineral cans and colourful Pizza Palace cartons littered the ground.

"It's the Brit," said Keith, rising to his feet. His flat-top hairstyle seemed to bristle with aggression. He had the same doughy complexion and full lips as his mother. "Get lost, Brit!" he growled. "You're trespassing on our scene."

"It's my grandfather's property," protested Tom. "You're the ones who are trespassing."

"You want to make something out of it?" sneered Keith, lifting his fists.

The other boys surrounded Tom, shoving him with their shoulders, poking him with their elbows. Tom pushed one of them away, causing him to stagger and bump into Keith.

"You made me hurt my friend," growled the boy. "I'm going to have to take your head off for that." Suddenly, he lashed out with his fist and hit Tom in his stomach.

As Tom staggered backwards, he heard a voice calling his name.

"Tom! Where are you?" Conor O'Carroll sounded near. "We're leaving now."

"Let's split," Keith hissed.

On one accord, the boys dashed from the shed. They climbed the wall and dropped over on to the embankment path.

"Beachwood brats," snapped Conor, looking at the litter on the floor. "The old man had stopped going out into the garden. That gang must have been coming here for months. I'll get the place cleared out and locked securely. Come on, Tom. It appears that your mother can't wait to shake the dust of Beachwood from her heels."

"Neither can I," gasped Tom, slowly beginning to breathe normally again.

The plane lifted into the air. Dinky cars seemed to move slowly along winding grey roads. The red roofs on tiny houses reminded him of the Lego towns he had built as a child. Then it nosed into the clouds and Tom, buried in cotton-wool mist, turned his face towards home.

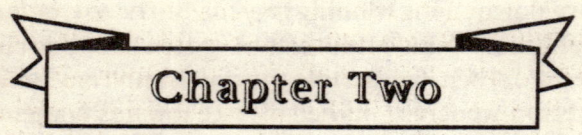

Chapter Two

Today we move to Ireland. This is the last time I'll hear old Mrs Thompson banging on her floor with her walking stick. Last night Lester and Jillian and Ola came to say goodbye. Jillian kissed me when she was leaving. First time. And wow! I don't want to go! Our flat has an echo. It's like an empty box and there's nowhere left to hide. We're leaving for Heathrow Airport in an hour. Why did he have to post that letter before he died?

The letter had been waiting for them when they arrived back at Ternville House. Helen recognised her father's handwriting and turned as pale as the envelope that lay on the floor. She checked the postmark. It had been posted on the day of his death. When she finished reading it, she handed it to her son. Then she leaned her hands on the kitchen counter and shouted, "Stupid, stupid man! Why did he have to leave it so late?"

Tom began to read the neat, slanting handwriting.

My daughter,

I have written this letter to you in my stubborn mind so many times over the past fourteen years that I know its contents off by heart. But everything I want to say is contained in these two words: forgive me.

Helen, I will die soon. This news was relayed to me by my trusted friend and doctor, John Darcy. I have no reason to doubt his word. He is always correct. He told me once that I would bitterly regret my unbending nature which drove you away and deprived me of the pleasure of knowing my grandchild.

But it is not too late to make amends. Suddenly, life seems so simple. Please come home and let me spend my last months with you and Tom. I know that your life has not been easy and that the ambitions you had as a young girl were pushed aside when Tom came into your life. After I die, I want you to remain in Mill Hill. Tom will have the opportunity to get in touch with the Irish side of his nature. My pride and stubbornness have denied him this right. As for you, Helen, go back to university to study as you had once hoped to do. I have sold my business so there will be money at your disposal. But even if you decide to turn down my offer, even if the bitterness between us runs too deep to be swept aside, allow me one last wish. To see your face and hold your hand once more before I die. Let me touch my grandchild. Let me be forgiven.

Write to me soon, my dear child.

"He must have posted it on his way to play golf," said Tom, carefully folding the letter into small pieces. He cleared his throat, nervously. "I'm glad he died before she got his letter," he thought, feeling utterly ashamed of himself for thinking such a terrible thing. But his main emotion remained one of relief that they were back in London and that Conor was selling the house on Mill Hill. Helen picked up her suitcase and walked quickly into her bedroom. The following week she told Tom they were moving to Beachwood.

"But why?" He was horrified.

"I have to go back to lay the ghosts, Tom," she said.

That was a most unsatisfactory answer, decided her son. But it was the only one he got. Over the next six months, his mother was busy. She contacted a university in Dublin about becoming a mature student, organised the shipping of their possessions to Ireland, gave in her notice to Techlore Trading, spent a lot of time talking on the phone to Conor O'Carroll and seemed to be filled with an energy and happiness that was in sharp contrast to Tom's growing dismay. One letter, posted fourteen years too late by a bitter old man, was changing his life, uprooting him from his home, his school, his friends, familiar places.

In May, Tom celebrated his fourteenth birthday with his friends Lester, Ola, Jillian, Naf-Naf and Andrew. He wondered with whom he would be celebrating when he became fifteen. The thought depressed him so much that he was silent throughout the film and afterwards, when they went to Chinatown for a Chinese meal, his appetite had disappeared. This was Helen's big treat. Tom walked past the restaurants and shops with their distinctive mouth-watering smells and rows of ducks hanging feet first in the windows. In two months time, London with its high, swanky houses and trendy sidestreets, its colourful market stalls and historical buildings, its teeming, hurrying population would be nothing more than a memory.

July arrived. At Heathrow Airport, they checked in at the Aer Lingus desk. In the duty free area, his mother suggested that he buy a present for Caro and Jennifer. "I'm sure they'd love some perfume or maybe skin cream." Helen was working hard at cheering him up. But Tom felt that his heart had turned into a painful lump that would rise up and choke him.

Conor met them at Dublin Airport. This time, there was no fierce hugging. Instead, Tom noticed a new easiness between the two adults as if they were friends from a long way back which, when he thought about it, was true. Helen had known Conor longer than she had known her son. In front of his eyes, Helen seemed to be changing from a quiet, serious woman into a giddy young girl who prefixed all her sentences with the words, "Conor, do you remember the time...?"

The house on Mill Hill looked as gloomy as he remembered. After Conor left, Helen opened the kitchen window. The distant chugging sound of a train reached his ears and faded.

"There's so much to be done." Helen smiled at him. "Between the two of us we'll shake every last cobweb from this place. We'll start redecorating immediately and have it all done before the end of the school holidays."

Tom could not get used to the idea that his mother was going back to college. She was going to do an Arts Degree in a place called University College Dublin while he would attend a school called Beachwood Comprehensive as a second-year student. He was not sure that he liked the sound of it at all.

"Tom! Don't look like that. You'll love Beachwood Comprehensive. It's my old school."

"You told me once that you hated it."

"I never!" she protested and started doing her "they were the best days of my life" routine.

Two months later the house had been redecorated and the summer holidays were at an end. He had seen Caro and Jennifer only twice since his arrival. Mill Hill was in the old part of Beachwood and quite a distance from Oaktree Estate where the girls lived. It was also too far to walk to Beachwood Comprehensive, so Helen bought him an Emmelle mountain bike and helmet for the journey. Helen had started driving lessons. Conor helped her choose a second-hand car. They had never owned a car before and Helen's driving terrified Tom. He kept pressing his foot down hard on an imaginary pedal and covering his face with his hands until she ordered him into the back seat because he was destroying her confidence. At the beginning of September, he wheeled his new bike down the driveway and waved goodbye to his mother. It was the first day of term.

Beachwood Comprehensive had once been a stately home. It still retained most of its historic features: heavy double-doors, a wide, high-ceilinged hall and flagstones covering the floor. The clatter of shoes was deafening. He felt uncomfortable in his school uniform. The first-year students looked apprehensive and stayed close together for protection. Throughout the summer months, they had terrified each other with horror stories about heads stuck down loos and bottoms glued to seats and canteen lunches dosed with pepper and legs tied to desks and underpants being ripped off and set on fire or hung, like trophies, from trees. The fact that they had never actually met anyone who had suffered those indignities made no difference. Everyone knew of someone who had been a victim.

To Tom, the pupils all looked and sounded alike. His school in London did not have a uniform and the pupils had been a rich mix of accents, colours and cultures. Only two of his friends, Lester and Jillian, had been true Londoners. The rest had been born or had roots in the West Indies, Scotland, Nigeria, Hungary and Japan.

Caro and Jennifer, looking neat and studious in their cream, beige and brown uniforms, introduced him to lots of their friends. Tom did not believe he would ever be able to remember their faces or the names of the teachers. Mrs Belton was his form tutor as well as his English teacher. She told him to report to her if he had any problems settling down.

"I taught your mother." At the start of her English class she smiled kindly at Tom. "Helen was an excellent pupil. I'm sure you're going to follow in her footsteps."

"Cor blimey, Miss!" said a voice, in an atrocious Cockney accent. "Did you teach his father as well?"

Without turning around, Tom knew that the voice belonged to Keith Fowler. He bent his head over the timetable that Mrs Belton had handed to him, feeling sick with embarrassment, knowing that everyone was watching him.

Mrs Belton frowned. "Who I taught or did not teach is of absolutely no concern to you, Keith Fowler," she snapped. "What should concern you is the standard of your school report, which left a lot to be desired. Perhaps, if you managed to pay attention this term to the things that concern you, there might be some chance of an improvement."

Caro and Jennifer giggled softly. They lowered their heads and twisted slyly around to stare at Keith, who glowered back. "Caroline Kane and Jennifer Hilliard! Pay attention immediately or I shall be forced to separate you. And this time it will be for good!" snapped Mrs Belton.

"Sorry, Miss," they replied, and turned sharply around to face her.

They brought Tom to the canteen for lunch. It was noisy with the rustle of lunch wrappings and the banging of trays. Many of the pupils had brought sandwiches but the canteen also supplied food. Tom joined the queue at the counter. It was much noisier and more unruly than the queue in his old school.

"Hey Parky! Wot you want to eat then, mite? Bangers and mash, eh?" Keith Fowler muscled in beside him. His jumper strained across his broad, stocky body.

"Why don't you push off and leave me alone," Tom suggested in his most polite voice.

"Cor blimey. 'E speaks proper English, 'e does. 'E's got an 'ot potato in his mouvh, 'e has!" gasped Keith. His three friends sniggered. One of them stood on each side of Tom and pushed against him, sandwiching him between them until he was forced to move out. His place in the queue immediately disappeared.

"You took my place!" he accused the boy who had been standing behind him.

"Did you 'ear that?" Keith appealed to the queue. "This Brit accused my mite of nicking 'is place, 'e did. Wot'll we do wiv 'im?"

Tom was getting very tired of Keith Fowler's accent, which sounded like a drunken imitation of the entire cast of "Eastenders." But he was the new boy in school. His sense of isolation made him nervous and homesick.

"Leave him alone, creep!" hissed Caro, who was standing in front of Keith. "Tom, come in here." She made a space for Tom and beckoned him in beside her.

"He's skipping the queue!" It was the boy who had punched Tom in his stomach in the shed at the bottom of his grandfather's garden.

Caro lowered her dark eyebrows and glared at him. "Why don't you push off and bully someone else, Liam Egan?" she snapped. "He's a new boy. The least you lot can do is make things easy for him."

"Ohhhh! Listen to 'er. 'E's 'er new boyfriend, 'e is," shouted Keith. His friends began to whistle and stamp their feet.

"Ignore them," ordered Caro. "They forgot to bring their soothers to school with them so they're getting restless."

"I see you met Ugly Egan and Freaky Fowler," said Jennifer, when they sat down beside her. Her loud voice carried effortlessly over the canteen. Tom wished he was invisible.

A boy called David sat beside them. Jennifer introduced him as her brother. Tom could see that there was something going on between David and Caro by the way they kept touching hands when they thought no one was looking. When a second boy pulled out a chair and sat down at their table, Tom blinked, wondering if he was suffering from double vision.

"Meet my twin, Michael." David grinned, obviously used to people's amazement when they met the twins for the first time.

"Double Trouble!" muttered Jennifer.

Michael wanted to talk to Tom about the Arsenal football team and last Saturday's game. He assumed that as Tom was from London he had to be an Arsenal fan.

"Arse Nil—Willie One," intoned David who followed Spurs and believed that Tom, he being an intelligent sort, would naturally frequent White Hart Lane. The twins jeered each other for a few minutes. Tom was unable to decide whether the "bandy-legged, short-sighted morons" that they were discussing played for Arsenal or Spurs. Jennifer kept chirping, "But what about the Dubs?" and Caro yawned, hugely. When Tom admitted that he was not interested in football and that he had never visited either Highbury Park or White Hart Lane, the twins looked amazed.

"What sort of sport do you play?" Michael asked.

"I'm not really into sport," Tom admitted, feeling that he had just failed his first test. "I'm into the environment and things like that."

"Oh!" Michael said. He brought a world of meaning to that one word. It dismissed Tom, dismissed his interests and firmly denied him any further attention from Michael Hilliard. He finished his lunch and wiped a hand across his mouth. "Catch you again, Tom. See you, girls."

"My brother Danny's mad into the environment as well," said Caro. "He drives us all mad talking about radioactive fishfingers."

"There he is. Danny! Over here!" yelled Jennifer and whistled sharply through two fingers. Every head in the canteen turned in her direction. "Come and meet Tom. He's another Eco Nut!"

Danny was a fourth-year student. He told Tom that he had recently formed an environmental rock band called Dancing on Grey Ash.

"It's a dreadful name," Caro insisted.

But Danny ignored her. He said that the name was symbolic of the near-destruction of the world and invited Tom to call to his house any time to see his environmental literature.

Tom was exhausted by the time the last class finished. When he entered the bicycle parking shelter he discovered that the tyres on his mountain bike were flat.

"Hey Parky! Wot's up? Ow, dearie me! 'E's got a flat tyre." Keith stood watching him, surrounded by his three friends.

"'Ave you not got your girlfriends to pump it up for you?"

"Did you let the air out of my tyres?" Tom demanded.

"Wot an 'orrible fing to fink!" Keith looked hurt.

"Are you accusing my mate of something?" asked Liam, raising his fists.

Tom ignored him and kept pumping, not looking up even when Liam aimed an accurate globule of spit at his shoes.

The boys walked on. Even when they were out of sight, Tom still imagined he could hear the mocking ring of their laughter ending his first day at Beachwood Comprehensive.

Chapter Three

My mother has started university. She is now officially a mature student. Mature! Huh! Her hair's cut like a boy's and she wears Docs and black leggings. She doesn't look like a mother any more. I'll die with embarrassment if she comes to a parent-teacher meeting like that. I've enough trouble to cope with. Beachwood Comprehensive is crap! Caro's OK and so's Jennifer. More than OK, actually, but I don't think she even notices me. I like Danny but he's in fourth year and hangs around with his own gang. There are Greenpeace posters all over the walls of his room. He's written a song called "Ivory Soul" which is about an elephant's tusks. He told me to enter the Beachwood Environmental Project Competition which is held at the end of term. I might do something on the rain forests. Mum's friend, Barry, has millions of photographs of plants and animals. I'll write and ask him to send me some. Danny gave me ECO News magazines and told me to join the ECO organisation.

It's to do with the environment. I might. At school everyone has their own crowd except me and that creep Fowler and his mates are still giving me a hard time. Fowler goes on and on with that stupid accent so much that I'm embarrassed to open my mouth. I miss Lester. I wrote to him twice but he still hasn't replied. Jillian sent me a letter with lipstick kisses all over her signature. Why did she have to wait until I left London to do things like that?

"'The Sex Woman' has arrived!" yelled Keith. This announcement was greeted by the boys with whistles and stamping feet.

"Dorks!" said Caro to Jennifer. "You'd think they'd grow up sometime."

Jenny Burrows was a brisk, no-nonsense type of woman, a counsellor who visited Beachwood Comprehensive once a year to give a series of lectures which she called "Living in Joy." They covered the areas of personal hygiene, friendship, healthy eating, physical exercise, study skills, emotional problems, mood swings, family relationships, puberty and girl–boy relationships. It was this latter subject which had earned her the unfortunate nickname of *The Sex Woman*. No matter what her talk was called, each time she gave a lecture the first- and second-year pupils settled down to listen in the hope of hearing fascinating things about sex that would introduce them into the mysterious world of adulthood. Afterwards, they always said: "We knew that bit already! or "That was *really* bor-ing!"

Today's lecture was entitled "Peer pressure and the influence it has on the lives of young people." It sounded interesting enough to gain Ms Burrows the full attention of 2A and 2B who had been herded into one room for her talk. Ms Burrows gave lots of examples as to how peer pressure worked. How it could be used to persuade young people to under-age drink, smoke, take drugs or have sex. To do anything that they did not wish to do but gave in and did because of pressure from their friends. She also asked them to examine the idea of "friendship" and what it meant to each of them. Then they had to distinguish the difference between friendship and peer group and to explain why it was so important to belong to the cool crowd.

Keith and his friends kept interrupting her, yawning and saying, "Miss, can you get to the interesting bit, *please!*"

Ms Burrows eyed them coldly and began to discuss the danger of peer pressure sex.

"Girls don't need any pressure," said Keith. "They love it."

His friends guffawed and nudged each other.

Aoife Johnston put up her hand. "Can I ask a question, Miss?"

When Ms Burrows nodded, Aoife sprang to her feet.

"How many boys present in this classroom would like to make love to their girlfriends before they get married?" she demanded.

For an instant the class was struck dumb with amazement. There was a certain amount of giggling and whispering before Keith Fowler shot up his hand. His friends immediately followed his example. Soon every boy in the room had his hand in the air. The girls began to mutter uneasily and shuffle in their seats.

"Now, let me ask another question," said Aoife, calmly. Her curly hair escaped from its hairband and frizzed around her forehead. "How many of you want to marry a girl who is a virgin?"

There was a gasp of outrage from the girls when every boy except Tom put up his hand.

A dangerous glint appeared in Aoife's eyes. "OK girls," she snapped. "Go get them."

Ms Burrows held up her hands to prevent a riot developing. "We will debate this issue in a civilised manner," she warned. "No violence, please!"

The discussion that followed was shrill and heated.

"One behaviour rule for the boys and one for the girls," shouted Jennifer. "That's the worst example of double standards I've ever seen."

"You lot are rotten," yelled Caro. She was flushed and angry. "All you want to do is get your own way. And if we do give in to you, you call us 'tarts' and if we don't, you say we're 'tight.' It's disgusting!"

"It's domination," stated Aoife who had started to read feminist literature. She had planned this scene ever since she heard the title of Ms Burrows' lecture. "It's a form of power control!"

"Stop getting so steamed-up!" A boy called Andrew Lee glared back at her. "It's no big deal. I just put up my hand because every other fellow did."

"Then that's even worse," shrilled Aoife, triumphantly. "That's peer pressure!"

"Right on!" yelled the girls, stamping their feet and thumping the boys next to them with their lecture sheets.

"Tom Parkinson is the only male non-chauvinist pig in this class!" Caro smiled with great fondness at him.

Tom slunk down in his desk. The boys, knowing that they were going to be roundly abused by the girls for the foreseeable future, glared scornfully at him.

"Would you like to tell us why you did not put up your hand, Tom?" asked Ms Burrows, doing him no favour at all.

"Why should we want it both ways? It...it's as Aoife said. It's a no-win situation for girls. And if they have a baby they shouldn't be left..." He looked down at the desk and felt the colour on his face sliding around to the back of his neck.

"He's right. We're the ones left holding the babies!" yelled Liz O'Rourke.

"Just like Helen Parkinson!" Keith Fowler's voice fell like a whip across the classroom. "That's what happened to her!"

Even Ms Burrows looked startled, her lips forming an O of shock in the silence that followed his words.

Andrew Lee tried to break the embarrassment with a joke. "What's all the fuss about?" he demanded. "There's nothing wrong with wanting to marry a Virgo."

"A Virgo!" Jennifer bellowed. "Pull the other one. That's not what you meant at all."

"What's your birth sign, Jennifer?" asked Liam Egan and some of the boys chanted, "Virgo! Virgo!"

Ms Burrows clapped her hands firmly and gradually the pupils settled down again. Tom sat with his head bowed while she devoted the rest of her lecture to the subject of considering other people's feelings. But the feelings of 2A and 2B were running high. She knew that no one was listening. When she left the classroom, her brisk walk was slower than usual and she shot a look of distaste at Keith who was lolling back in his desk, examining his nails.

"Tom! Wait for us." He was wheeling his bike out of

the school grounds when Caro and Jennifer caught up with him.

"Thanks for what you did back there," said Caro. "You really showed those jerks up."

"It won't help my popularity," he replied, ruefully.

Keith, Liam and Oliver Kerr walked past. "'Ello Virgos," Keith drawled, staring at Tom. "Are we 'aving a little gossip about peer pressure?"

"We're either tight or tarts," Liam chanted in a falsetto voice.

"Get lost!" retorted Jennifer.

The boys walked on in front and disappeared around the bend in the path.

"Don't mind them," advised Caro. "They're just show-offs. Not all the boys are like Keith. But he has a following of airheads and whatever he says, goes."

Tom had already noticed this. Keith was the leader of the pack. Even boys who were not part of his gang made no effort to befriend Tom because they knew that Keith would jeer at them if they did. They either ignored him or looked embarrassed if he tried to talk to them. It was as if Keith had hung a label around his neck with the word "wimp" written on it and that was all the boys saw.

"Are you making any friends?" Helen asked him that evening. She was anxious about Tom and unable to understand why he had so little to say about his new school except, "It's all right."

"You *are* happy, Tom? You're not sorry we moved?" Her smile was strained. He knew she wanted him to be content in his new surroundings.

"Of course I'm happy," he said and watched the tension ease from her face. Tom felt as if he had grown very old since he came to live in Beachwood but his mother seemed to become younger with each passing week. It was as if their time together was sliding by on a conveyor belt, not stopping long enough for them to talk any more, at least not the way they did in the old days. Each evening, they studied together. It had been fun at first but his mother's new friends from university kept ringing her and she would spend ages on the phone talking about lectures and tutorials and booklists. Mornings were a flurry of activity as they both did their chores before leaving the house.

In London, she had been his closest friend. His school friends had lived too far away to visit after school hours and there were no young people of his age in Ternville House. The city had never ceased to fascinate Helen and she had brought Tom to see all the historical sights, London Bridge, the Tower, Buckingham Palace, the museums and art galleries. They used to eat in Covent Garden, watch the young people strutting along the King's Road in their way-out clothes on Saturday mornings and listen to the soapbox speakers on Hyde Corner.

"I am the tourist who never goes home." His mother would laugh, a bright, high sound, and he would wonder what she meant. To him, his mother was London. It had been impossible to imagine her in any other setting. Yet since their return to Ireland, he realised how desperately she had wanted to come home throughout those years when she had been building a sense of identity for her son in another country.

Chapter Four

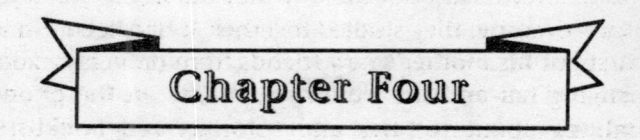

I helped Stinger Muldoon today, Saturday. He's a fisherman with an ugly dog called Beethoven but he does odd jobs around the village. We cut back the branches from the big trees in the back garden. I can now see the embankment quite clearly. I'm going to climb down there some day. Just like my father! That's my challenge. I've got to get over my fear of heights, especially as Mr Brown (Geography) has promised to bring us abseiling. I've seen it done on telly. All these soldiers slid down the side of a cliff on a rope. It made me dizzy just to look at them. We're doing it in a place called Howth Head. Can't give in. Caro says she's going to arrange it so that I get to sit beside Jennifer on the bus. My mother's gone for a really posh meal in a place called The Zany Crowe's Nest with Conor tonight. I think he fancies her...

Tom stopped writing in his diary for a moment to see what effect that last unfinished sentence had on him. To his relief, he felt no pangs of jealousy. He liked Conor, who ran the riding school with Mrs O'Carroll, his mother. He had offered to teach Tom to ride. But, after two lessons, Tom had declined to continue. He was nervous and awkward on horseback. The mare, sensing his fear, had tossed her head and made loud, trumpeting sounds that had turned Tom's blood to ice. She had stopped suddenly to eat grass that seemed to grow very far down from where Tom was sitting. His orders for her to move were ignored. Yet as soon as Conor uttered the softest of commands, she had plodded home like a tame lamb.

"Don't worry, Tom. It's all too new." Conor had tried to console him. "New country, new people, new school, new hobbies. Give yourself time to settle down and we'll try again."

Tom knew he would not try again. But he was determined to make a success of abseiling. He turned a page in his diary and paused when he heard the sound of a door slamming. It came from the direction of the back garden. When he looked out of his bedroom window, he had a clear view of the wooden shed. Flickering torchlight beamed from the window.

"I'm going to throw them out," he growled. His anger gave him courage. The neatly-clipped bushes were still high enough to keep him out of sight. A gust of wind shook the branches and whipped fallen leaves across the crazy pavement. He heard Liam Egan's voice, followed by raucous laughter.

He wanted to smash open the door and kick them out, one by one. But he was scared, remembering the last time he had disturbed them. Outside the door, he hesitated. Suddenly it opened and he found himself facing the torch. The beam was so strong that he was staring into a round black void. He recognised Keith Fowler's voice.

"It's the Brit. He's spying on us." Keith was so startled that he forgot to put on his Cockney accent. He grabbed Tom and pulled him into the shed. The wind, blowing wild, slammed the door behind him, repeating the noise that had first alerted Tom. Cigarette smoke hazed the air and there was a tangy smell of chips and vinegar. Tom figured there were seven or eight boys sitting on wooden boxes or sprawled on the floor.

"You've no right to be in here," he said, trying to keep his voice steady.

Keith twisted the neck of Tom's sweatshirt in his fist and the smaller boy gasped as the material tightened on his throat. "You say one word about this and we'll never let you forget it," said Keith. "Understand, Brit!"

Suddenly the shrill call of a police siren made everyone jump with shock. It drew nearer, travelling fast up Mill Hill.

"You called the police!" Keith hissed. "You sneaky little shit!"

Tom staggered against the door when Keith released his grip. The boys were panic-stricken. They rushed past Tom and began to climb the back garden wall.

"You'll pay for this." Keith was the last to leave. "Just you wait. You'll pay."

"I didn't call the police!" Tom's cry was lost in the darkness as Keith vaulted like a cat over the wall and disappeared.

Two policemen stood at the front door. They told Tom that they'd received a phone call from a neighbour who claimed to have seen boys climbing over the back wall. "We know that kids sometimes hung around here when the place was empty," said a young man called

Garda O'Hara. "Let's take a look." He switched on the shed light and pursed his lips when he saw the white chip papers and cigarette butts. "Have you heard anything or seen any of them?" he asked Tom.

Tom shook his head.

"Well, if you do, give us a ring immediately," said Garda O'Hara. "Sergeant Hilliard will soon sort them out."

Monday morning was wet and miserable. A typical start-of-the-week blues day. Misty October rain steamed the windows. The muggy heat of the classroom made everyone listless and inattentive. Mrs Belton became so impatient with them that for homework she gave them a six-hundred-word English essay on "The Importance of Being Earnest and Attentive in Class."

After lunch, Tom went into the science room and seated himself on a vacant stool. Just before Mrs McColl, the science teacher, arrived, Keith hooked his foot into the lower rung of his stool and yanked it out from under him. With his arms folded on the worktop bench, Tom was taken by surprise. He tumbled forward, hitting his chin off the worktop as he fell. When he got to his feet, Keith was crouched before him, making "take me on" gestures with his hands.

"You stupid dork, Keith Fowler!" Caro sprang down from her stool and rushed to separate them.

"Give him a big kiss and make him better, Caro," sneered Duane Ryder, another member of Keith's gang. Some of the boys began to laugh.

"Belt up, Duane!" She blushed and looked embarrassed. "Can't you just leave him alone?"

Ashamed of the jeering he received whenever Caro or Jennifer tried to defend him, Tom brushed her aside and snapped, "Back off, Caro! I don't need a minder!"

"There's no need to be so standoffish. I was only trying to help." Caro stomped back to her desk, her cheeks pink with indignation. A warning growl from Oliver Kerr told them that Mrs McColl was on her way. Everyone settled into positions of attention as the door opened.

That anybody should dislike him so viciously was a new experience for Tom and one that filled him with an uneasy sense of shame. He knew very little about bullying. He had never been a bully nor, in his fourteen years, had he ever been the victim of one. But he was learning all about it: the taunting in class and the name-calling, the loneliness of being the outsider, the flat tyres and the deep scrape along the neon paintwork of his mountain bike, the journey home alone from school and the fear that he would be waylaid and beaten on the way. It was like a poison, this creeping sense of being ridiculed. The other boys in 2B ignored him as if he would taint them with his unpopularity. Sometimes, in those first fuzzy early moments between dreams and sleep, Tom would think he was back again in London. Then he would remember and the day, with all its fears and misery, seemed to stretch endlessly before him. He tried to keep his head down and attract as little attention as possible. After school, he spent his time in his room, putting together his project on the destruction of the rain forests which he called "The Chain Saw Massacre." The title suited his mood.

Chapter Five

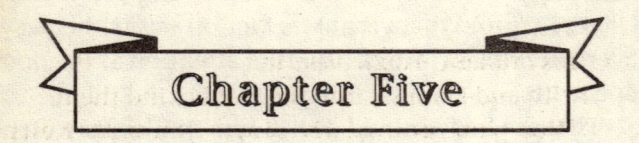

*T*oday's the day. Abseiling. I feel sick. Please God, don't let me mess it up!

Tom sat by himself on the bus. Jennifer and Caro ignored him but, as Jennifer passed his seat, she plonked down beside him.

"Hi Jennifer," he said.

The blonde girl started with surprise and appeared to notice him for the first time.

"Oh! Hi. I didn't know you were coming with us."

"Why shouldn't I?"

"I thought we were supposed to back off and let you get on with your life."

"Things have been a bit rough…"

"So I noticed." She looked sympathetically at him. "You must hate Beachwood."

"There are some things that make it *very* worthwhile."

"Such as?" she challenged him, knowing exactly what he meant.

"You and Caro. But especially you."

"Chancer. I don't believe a word of it." She tossed her hair back from her shoulders. "Is this your first time abseiling?"

"Yes."

"It's brilliant. You'll *adore* it."

Keith and Liam sat into the seat behind them.

"Wot you doing wiv 'im, Jenny?" Keith's interpretation of a London accent was not improving with practice. "'E's a Brit, 'e is. Wot's wrong wiv us lot then, huh?"

"Why don't you bury your face in a rock, creep!" shouted Jennifer without turning around. Tom was beginning to believe that Jennifer could shout down a hurricane. Her words effortlessly reached Mr Brown. The teacher was sitting in the front of the bus with three of his rock-climbing friends, who had come along to help out.

"Be quiet," he roared. "If you don't learn to modulate your voice, Miss Hilliard, you'll be banned from abseiling. I've no intention of starting a rock slide."

"That's not fair, sir. Keith Fowler started it."

"Me, sir?" In amazement, Keith flung himself back in his seat. "I said nothing."

"He did, sir. He kept *saying* things!" Jennifer was furious.

"Would you like to repeat what he said?" demanded Mr Brown.

Jennifer slumped her shoulders and turned bright red. "No sir."

"Then utter one more word and you're out of the team," Mr Brown warned her.

For the remainder of the journey, the two boys exchanged remarks about Jennifer and Tom "getting off" in low voices that only the embarrassed couple in front of them could hear. Once, when Tom jerked around in fury and hissed at Keith to "zip his lips," Jennifer pulled him sharply by his arm. "Don't make waves," she muttered. "They're not worth it."

It was a sharp but sunny October afternoon. The scent of woodsmoke drifted past the young people as they climbed up slippery wooden steps built into the hillside. Granite rocks bulged out of the ground and the dying, yellowing ferns were knee-high. Jennifer slipped once and Tom was able to hold her hand for an instant until she regained her balance. Caro walked with them and no longer had a snooty expression on her face. Upwards they climbed, stepping over tree roots and a golden carpet of dead leaves. Then they were looking down on a thick crown of tree tops. Across Dublin Bay, they could see the high red chimneys of the Pigeon House. The sea glinted in the autumn sunlight as if silver needles danced over the waves.

They finally stopped at the edge of a sheer crag face. The wind was sharp on the exposed ledge.

The young people milled around Mr Brown and his rock-climbing assistants. Those who had abseiled before were showing off, demanding to be the first down the sheer crag face. Finally the shouting and bedlam died down. Mr Brown split the students into groups of five. Caro, Keith, Liam, Jennifer and Tom were in his group. Tom kept looking at the equipment piled at his feet because if he looked over the edge of the rock face, a tickling sick feeling swayed in the pit of his stomach. He felt as if he was losing his sense of balance and wanted to lie down on the grass beneath his feet, to bury his face in the strong, springy roots. To do anything other than face the fact that in a few minutes he would be sliding over the edge of an abyss, hurtling into the arms of death.

Liam had noticed the putty-like colour of his face. An experienced abseiler, he knew the signs of a novice and nudged Keith.

"Hey Parky, abseiling is the one area of rock climbing where the most accidents occur," remarked Keith.

"Do you remember that time when my cable broke and I was hanging by a single strand?" said Liam. "I was that close to death!" He made a minuscule space between his thumb and index finger.

"What a pity I didn't have a scissors handy," snarled Jennifer.

"Harmony is essential in a rock-climbing team. Are we happy together?" demanded Mr Brown.

"Yes sir," they chorused.

Keith was Mr Brown's star pupil. He would go first and demonstrate the simplicity of abseiling. His eyebrows jutted aggressively beneath his climbing helmet. He deftly fastened on a harness with loops and buckles, fastening it around him with the assurance of one who does rock climbing in his sleep. Then he uncoiled his rope, running it carefully through his hands, inspecting it for any sign of damage. He looked impressive in his colourful climbing gear and rock boots. Tom's stomach heaved again as he watched Keith leaning backwards and beginning his descent. The others followed, screeching with excitement when they reached the bottom. One by one they reappeared, climbing back up the crag trail, looking flushed and exhilarated.

At last, Mr Brown turned to Tom. "Are you feeling OK, lad?" he asked brusquely.

Miserably, Tom nodded.

"Abseiling is a fun experience. What is it, Tom?"

"A fun experience, sir," whispered Tom.

Mr Brown showed him how to fix his harness, to fix the abseil rope to a device on the harness called a figure of eight. Tom was horrified. His life depended on a thing that looked as fragile as the ring on a beer can.

The geography teacher roared with laughter at Tom's description. "Just relax. You'll enjoy it. Remember what I said. It's a fun experience." Mr Brown slapped him on his back. He had a hearty manner and was a brisk, sporty man who believed that fresh air and guts took care of all of life's problems. "Once you go over the edge, don't let your buttocks drop lower than your feet or you'll flip over backwards."

"What!" Tom's voice was a faint whine.

"Don't worry if that happens. You'll be able to right yourself quickly enough. And I have a safety rope so you're doubly protected. Now, remember, keep your feet flat against the crag face all the way down."

Tom thought his heart would stop beating as he lowered himself over the edge, feeling his legs tense with pressure. Slowly one foot followed the other. He began to increase his speed. Sweat smeared his forehead. He leaned out too far and, suddenly, he was flipping backwards and hanging upside down, his descent abruptly halted. The rocks spun and blurred. The wind was a mad lament, shrieking around his face, ready to whip him into eternity.

Mr Brown was talking to him, giving him clear instructions, ordering him to stay calm. Tom whimpered and instinctively swung clockwise and back into an upright position. He remembered Liam's story about the single rope strand. He could hear the strands on his cable snapping, one after the other until only a cobweb held him upright. He saw the safety rope.

"Don't let go of the abseil cable," yelled Mr Brown. "You're perfectly safe."

But Tom, sobbing hysterically, released it and grabbed the safety rope. This rope, more flexible than the abseil cable, bounced slightly and he felt himself dropping even further. His scream bounced off the crag face and the entire class of 2B stared down at him.

"OK! You're all right. I'll take you up." Mr Brown sounded disgusted.

Tom collapsed on the grass. Mr Brown told him to press his head between his knees. Gradually the sky and the rocks stopped spinning around him in a mad orbit.

"Imagine freaking out like that. Even a baby could do that crag," scoffed Keith.

"Button your lip, Fowler," snapped Mr Brown. But Tom knew that his geography teacher agreed with Keith. He glanced up at Jennifer. She smiled kindly at him. He imagined that she would look upon the body of a drowned kitten with the same pity. It was not at all the kind of emotion he had hoped to arouse in her. He placed his head back between his knees again and gathered his misery tightly around him.

Chapter Six

*R*otten day. Everyone in school knows about the abseiling. Probably the whole village knows. Heck! Why not the world? Hey, out there. Just in case you haven't heard, Parky's a coward! In PE today, Keith Fowler kept hanging upside down and shouting in a really high voice: "Help! I'm falling! Help! Save me, Jennifer!" His friends thought he was so funny! Stupid jerks. I hate them. Even some of the girls were laughing. Jennifer says they're sick and not to mind them. But I bet she's laughing behind my back too! My project on the rain forests is going well. I've done a section on the monkeys that live there. I've drawn pictures of them jumping from tree to tree. They're not scared of heights. Tomorrow is my half-day. I'm going to climb down the embankment as soon as I get home from school.

In London, Tom had used the underground regularly. He

had been familiar with the echoing platforms where people rushed in and out of tubes and up and down the escalators as if mad dogs were snapping at their heels. Sometimes, a little mouse would scurry between the sleepers on the tracks. It always amazed Tom that such a frail life could survive in the shuddering, noisy life of a tube station. Each time this happened, he believed it was the same mouse but Lester used to scoff and tell him not to be so soft.

Beachwood railway station was a quiet platform with potted shrubs and a ticket collector who knew everyone's name. Beyond the station, the railway tracks ran over Swansbury Estuary where a man-built bank of earth and a viaduct stretched across the water. Then the land became hilly and the tracks passed through a narrow valley with high embankments on each side. This was Mill Hill territory.

Tom climbed the garden wall and stood on top of the embankment. He looked down at the railway tracks far below. The path was fenced with barbed wire and a large notice warned: *Danger. No Climbing Allowed*. He glanced quickly around and lifted the wire.

In summer, the top of this embankment was a blaze of yellow ragwort but as autumn drew to a close it left a toll of dead weeds behind. Even the grass had a dog-eared look, flattened and yellowed like the turned pages of an old book. Half-way down, the land suddenly stopped as if a giant spade had sliced the earth cleanly away to reveal a rock face. This created a long drop to an incline below which was covered with sandy gravel. A dead tree spread its withered branches and stood like a scrunched old crone guarding the railway tracks. With his eyes, Tom measured the climb he must make. He sat down abruptly on the grass, gritting his teeth and muttering, "Coward...coward...coward!" He had been saying that one word to himself ever since he returned from Howth Head.

He turned his back on the railway tracks and began his descent, clinging to clumps of grass and the roots of bushes that coiled above the earth. The rock face was as far as he intended going. By the time he reached it, his nails had broken and the knuckles on one hand were bleeding. Anchoring his feet to a thick clump of grass, he cautiously turned around. What had looked like a sheer rock face from the top of the embankment was now revealed as a surface with crevices and jutting pieces of flint. Handholds and footholds.

"No!" wailed a small voice inside his mind. "Don't be daft! You've done enough for one day." But he was already lowering himself over the edge. This was more difficult than the soft grassy climb. Half-way down, he knew he had made a mistake. His foot searched blindly behind him for a hold. His hands gripped a rough crevice and he prayed that he could continue, that he would not freeze as he had done on Howth Head. This time there was no cable, no safety rope, nothing but the sheer drop to the tracks below. But there was also the knowledge that his father had once made this climb and when his toes fitted snugly into a narrow ledge, he wondered if his father had also paused breathlessly in the same position. His heart was beating so loudly that when he heard the distant sound growing louder and louder, he did not realise it was a train. Then the embankment became alive with a hammering, clattering, whistling roar. It seemed to last forever. His body pressed flat against the rock face. There was a gritty feeling in his eyes as sandy gravel flew upwards in clouds of dust. The sound grew to a climax and just when he believed he could no longer hold on, it passed and became a fading beat of steel upon steel, heading towards Dublin city.

Cautiously, he began to move. The silence after the train had a calming effect on him and he grew more confident. The land began to slope beneath him and he was on the last stage of the climb. He was able to face the tracks and, as his feet slid on the loose gravel, he used the seat of his jeans as a toboggan to reach the bottom. He sat beneath the branches of the dead tree, a hawthorn that had once showered the tracks with white May blossom. For a moment he did not feel any emotion except a numbing sense of peace. He hugged his knees and watched a flock of birds scattering like confetti across the evening sky. Then, slowly, he turned around and looked back. High and severe, the embankment loomed above him. He had climbed it, descended into his fear and conquered it. The fact that there was no one there to watch him made no difference. In time, he would show them.

The next train was not due for a half-hour. As he jumped over the sleepers, he wondered how the London mouse had known when it was safe to surface between trains and scamper along the tracks. Maybe Lester was right and each time it was a different mouse, too stupid to learn from the squashed fate of previous mice. The thought depressed him and he began to sing a song about a mouse who wore clogs and hung around the stairs all the time. His mother used to sing it to him when he was little but he could no longer remember the words. She would faint if she knew he had climbed down the embankment. The thought of causing such shock and horror pleased him. Maybe he would tell Jennifer. Maybe he would even bring her to the embankment and demonstrate his climbing skills. Reclaim his image!

He walked for a long time and did not notice twilight setting around him. The five o'clock express whistled past. He stayed far back from the tracks yet its speed and the blast of air it created almost sucked him forward. After the sounds faded, he heard the raucous screech of seagulls flying low over Swansbury Estuary. There would be people on Swansbury Road and he would be in full view. Sergeant Hilliard took a very dim view of young people disobeying the notices that warned against trespassing on the tracks. Time for fade-out action.

The banks of earth on each side had flattened and were easy to climb. Rows of houses stretched along the top, cordoned off by brown, wooden fences. If he could run through a garden, it would bring him out in one of the housing estates and he would be able to find his way back to Mill Hill. Gaps in the fences revealed tidy lawns, offering him little shelter. Further along, he saw a wilderness of high grass. The house looked deserted with drawn curtains and a general air of neglect hanging over it. Tom climbed the fence and prepared to sprint towards the side passage that would bring him to the front of the house. He had reached the back door when an outside light flashed on and froze him in its glow. The door opened slowly.

The woman who stood facing him was old. Tom figured she had to be a hundred at the very least. Her bulky, hunched figure reminded him of the dead tree on the embankment. She wore layers of clothes, a jumper, cardigan, a faded yellow anorak and trousers tucked into moon boots. Before he could move, she had reached him.

Her fingers gripped his arm and her eyes glittered with determination.

"It's the police for you, my boy. I've had enough nonsense from the lot of you, breaking my windows and throwing bangers through my letterbox."

"I wasn't doing anything! Honest!" He was terrified of the stern face with the beaky nose and clenched mouth. Her grip was strong, holding on even when he tried to wrench free. But he was stronger and her fingers soon began to loosen. Her hand slid helplessly to her side. Yet she still stood squarely before him and blocked his path. He wanted to push her away. It would have been an easy thing to do. But she reminded him of Mrs Thompson who had lived in the flat above him in London, a cranky, fierce, old woman who complained about everything he did but had wept into his chest when he said goodbye to her.

"Please, let me pass. I was only taking a short-cut through your garden."

"A likely story. The police are on their way. You'll be sent to jail." She smirked, triumphantly. Suddenly, her gaze focused directly on Tom as if, until that instant, she had seen him only as a faceless hooligan whose main purpose in life was to annoy her. She shivered and staggered to one side. Afraid that she would fall, Tom forced himself to touch her, to hold her steady, to lead her back into her house. She did not protest. All the fight and vigour seemed to have left her. A naked bulb burned brightly from the kitchen ceiling. The room was freezing. Dirty dishes were piled in the sink and the tablecloth looked as if it had not been shaken or washed for weeks. She slumped into a chair and muttered: "You're not him. I thought for a moment...time is such a cruel thing...cruel...cruel. It doesn't make sense to me any more."

Tom was poised to flee. "I have to go. My mother..."

"You're not like the other boys." She interrupted him. "They think they can frighten me. Ha! I send them running with their bangers and their rude words. In my day we had respect for old people. Do you know what age I am?" she asked.

"Seventy-five," answered Tom, diplomatically.

"Eighty-four," she boasted. "And I'm still able to look after myself. My daughter went away, you know. Selfish girl. She was all I had. Then I had Thomas. But only for a little while. Sit down, boy. I must make you some tea. A growing boy like you has to eat properly. I'm going to boil you an egg. A nice big egg for a growing boy."

"She's mad. Totally bats!" Tom was petrified as the old woman began to hum and open presses. Under the light, her scalp was pink beneath wispy grey hair.

"I can't stay. My mother will be wondering..."

"There you are now. A knife and a spoon." She took the cutlery from the basin of unwashed dishes and rubbed them with a grubby towel. "It's a long time since I've had anyone to tea. Not since Thomas."

The egg boiled. Water overflowed, hissing and spitting on the cooker. Steam ran down the window and closed off the evening.

"Eat up," ordered the woman. She sliced the top off his egg.

"I don't like boiled..."

She sat opposite him and glared. "Come on, now. It's good for you. Thomas always ate my boiled eggs." Her mouth quivered.

"Oh no! She's going to cry," Tom looked with

desperate longing towards the back door. He spooned some egg into his mouth, hoping to please her. The egg was hard and rubbery. He chewed and rolled his eyes in appreciation. But she was looking over his shoulder and after a moment her eyes closed. "I've done an awful thing." She seemed to be talking to herself. "I dream about it at night. I want Thomas. I have to tell him..." Her words died away and she opened her eyes. "I'm all alone, boy. All alone."

"Doesn't your daughter ever visit you?" Tom felt the chill of the kitchen numbing his toes.

"She died." Her voice had grown weak and quavery. "She went away and then she died. Now there's only Thomas. He sends me money, you know. But he won't come. I won't let him."

"Does he live in Beachwood?"

"Beachwood! Huh! Beachwood was not good enough for my daughter. Australia! That's where she went. And then Thomas was born. She gave me only one grandchild. Selfish girl, to go and die on me like that."

Tom's throat felt dry. It hurt when he spoke. "Are you Mrs Maxwell?"

She hesitated, her monologue interrupted. "Why do you want to know?"

"My name is—"

"No!" The faded eyes narrowed, filled with dread and suspicion. She drew her shoulders up high so that her head was almost buried in the thick anorak. "Go away, boy. You're making my head ache." Tears ran down her furrowed cheeks. "Go away! Go away...before I call the police!"

Tom closed the door on her words. He stumbled through the dark hall and out the front door. As he walked back to Mill Hill, he kept his eyes on the ground, knowing that for the second time, his great-grandmother had refused to recognise his existence. When Keith and his gang, slouching against the wall of The Greasy Spoon, shouted across the road at him, he did not even hear them. "Jennifer!" they chanted. "Save me. I'm fallll...inggg!"

Chapter Seven

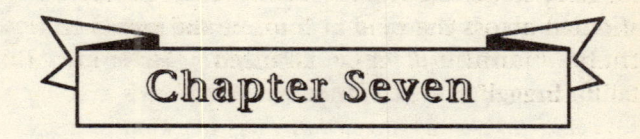

It was a really strange feeling to discover I have a great-grandmother. I like the sound of that word. She's the first relation I've even met, except for my grandfather, but he wasn't into anything but the angels when we finally did get together. I saw her again today. I was in the supermarket with Mum when she appeared at the other end of the aisle, scrunched up over her trolley and looking real mean. Mum immediately started examining the price on a jar of marmalade and didn't look up until my great-grandmother had passed. She ignored us but I could feel her beady little eyes examining the back of my neck. I asked Mum who she was and she gave me a sideways stare. Her voice sounded choked off when she said, "No one you need to know." Then she went up to the cash desk even though there were loads of things still on the shopping list. On the way home I told Mum that I believed the old woman was my great-grandmother. Mum nearly crashed the car and began ranting on *about me having nothing to do with her. I never saw her in such a temper. I hope she doesn't find out I've been to my great-grandmother's house. Tonight I asked her if she had loved my father. I never thought much about that part of the story until I came to Beachwood. Now I think about it all the time. She said I was a love child and no matter what had happened afterwards, nothing could take away from that fact. It's kind of sick-making stuff but nice. I've no intention of going to visit my great-grandmother ever again. She scares the wits out of me. I wonder would she say anything about my father? Crabby old bat. I'd be the last person she'd talk to about him.*

It was Caro who gave Tom the idea when she told him about the Teeny-Moppers, a group of young people who did jobs for elderly people in Beachwood. Mrs Boggan's cottage in Bowman's Lane was their flagship. It gleamed with fresh paint and trimmed gardens, back and front. Caro told him (after first swearing him to secrecy) that they had started looking after the bungalow as a result of a slumber party she and her friends had had during the summer. They owed Mrs Boggan a debt of gratitude because she had saved them from trouble when they were discovered out of doors on that wild night. Caro told Tom that Mrs Boggan belonged to a group called The Celtic Seekers After Psychic Knowledge. She had been checking out psychic vibrations in Hobourne Park with Professor Price, an expert on all things ghostly, when she came upon Caro and her friends.

"That's what they told us. But I think they were just having a snog," Jennifer had chimed in. Caro looked disgusted and said that Jennifer was incapable of thinking about anything else. Tom hoped that was true especially when Jennifer lifted her eyebrows quizzically at him. Mrs Boggan's well-maintained bungalow had given him an idea.

"Why don't you call on Mrs Maxwell?" he asked. "I'd go with you and give a hand."

Jennifer threw up her hands and moaned. "That crabby old witch. No way!"

"She's always ringing the police and complaining about us," Caro added. "Even when we called and offered to tidy up her place, she screamed at us."

"And she's always stealing footballs," said Jennifer. "If they get kicked into her garden by accident, she never gives them back. My brothers believe that she has one room in her house that holds nothing but Hilliard footballs."

"It was just a thought," said Tom. "Forget it."

He called to Elmtree Close the following day. When Mrs Maxwell opened her front door she left just enough width for one baleful eye to peer out.

"Go away!" she snapped in her quavering old voice. "I'm not buying raffle tickets or sponsoring jogs. And tell the rest of your friends not to dare ring my doorbell again."

"It's me, Mrs Maxwell. We met last week. Can I come in?"

"You!" The door opened another fraction and he could see her more clearly. A withered tree. The analogy came back to his mind again. A thorn tree, prickly and impossible to touch. "How dare you come to my house! I'm going to call Sergeant Hilliard and have you arrested."

"I came only because I thought you might like some help in the house."

"Help! What do you mean, help? I'm well able to take

care of myself. Go away from here this instant, you cheeky brat! And make sure you close the gate properly." She slammed the door in his face.

"I hate her," he raged. "I'll never go near her again. Never! Never again!"

It was a week before he called again, his mind turning back with every forward step he took.

"Why am I doing this?" he muttered. "I'm getting enough abuse from Freaky Fowler and his mob without this hassle!"

There was no answer to his ring on the doorbell. He was about to leave when his attention was caught by a bottle of milk, delivered that morning and tucked into a narrow alcove in the porch. A bird had found it and tapped through the tinfoil top. Droplets of milk stained the tiled porch. Maybe Mrs Maxwell had gone away. He remembered her half-defiant, half-plaintive cry that she had nobody and did not need anybody. He walked around the side of the house and tried to peer in the kitchen window. The kitchen was as untidy as on his first visit. The dining room windows were covered in grime. He used a paper handkerchief to clear a patch of glass and, peering through, saw a bed beside the opposite wall. It was heaped high with blankets. For an instant, it was difficult to see if anyone was lying in it. Then he saw her hair. The fingers of one hand clutched the top of the bedclothes. Her humped figure underneath was perfectly still. Tom was half-way towards the front gate before he forced himself to stop. He had to return and help her.

"Maybe she's dead," he kept repeating and felt a shudder of dread running all the way to his toes.

The garage door was an up-and-over type. When he twisted the handle, it opened. At the end of the garage, a side door led into the house but this was securely locked. He found a long, rusting screwdriver and went around again to the back of the house. The wood on the dining room window was rotting and, hooking his fingers underneath the jutting ledge of the frame, he began to pull. It gave way slightly. He was able to slide the screwdriver through the narrow gap and force up the clasp. Finally, it burst open and he climbed through.

A faint smell of Vicks and medicine, stale smoke, perspiration, the smell of neglect, Tom was conscious of all of these things. Yet they did not register on his mind as he approached the bed. How tiny she looked. He heard a faint wheezy sound and, shaky with relief, dropped to his knees at the side of the bed. The beady, faded eyes opened, lit for an instant with gratitude before hazing back into unconsciousness.

Out in the hall he found a telephone and, in the front page of the telephone directory, Dr Darcy's number. Dr Darcy asked a few brisk questions and promised to come immediately. A dusty address book lay beside the directory. Tom's hands shook as he turned the pages and saw the name Thomas O'Meara. The address underneath the name was in Melbourne. The letters blurred before his eyes. Quickly, he tore out the page and stuffed it into the back pocket of his jeans.

By the time Dr Darcy arrived, Mrs Maxwell had recovered consciousness.

"OK, Beautiful, let's have a look at you." The doctor carried a briefcase which he called "his bag of tricks." He jollied Mrs Maxwell into emerging from beneath the bedclothes so that her chest could be examined and shook his head ruefully as he listened to her shallow breathing.

"Well, Beautiful, despite your best efforts, you're not going to die on us this time." He took her blood pressure, gave her an injection and scolded her in a jocular but gentle way. "What do you think I am? A parrot? Is my mission in life to go around repeating the same things to you over and over again? What did I say the last time? Contact me as soon as you feel the slightest wheeze in your chest. Get in Meals on Wheels. Get a home help. Talk to your neighbours. But do you ever listen to one word I say? Only for this young man here, God knows what would have happened to you."

Mrs Maxwell was too ill to argue back. Her waxy skin reminded Tom of his grandfather's body, but her eyes settled on him in a greedy gaze that he found most unnerving.

"He's Thomas. My grandson. He's come from Australia to look after me," she wheezed.

"You need looking after, right enough." Dr Darcy carefully settled the bedclothes around her shoulders and beckoned Tom to accompany him outside.

"Who exactly are you?" he asked.

"Tom Parkinson."

"Ahhh! I see. Helen Parkinson's son. That brings me back a few years. A lovely young girl. I heard she was back in Beachwood. How did you discover Mrs Maxwell?"

Tom told him what happened. The doctor listened attentively, throwing in the occasional casual question so that by the time Tom finished speaking, he knew about the previous meetings and had guessed the rest.

"Does Helen know you come here?"

Tom stared at the ground. "Not exactly."

"Does that mean she would have a freak if she knew?" asked Dr Darcy, shrewdly.

Tom shuffled his feet and nodded. He liked Dr Darcy. When he heard how Tom had had to force the window to gain entry, he frowned. "Mrs Maxwell is suffering from severe pneumonia. Her neighbours are at work during the day and she's fought with every one of them so they have no great desire to call on her. If you hadn't come along, it's very likely she would have died."

"What about her family?" Tom studied a damp piece of wallpaper above the doctor's head. "Why don't they take care of her? It's not right to leave her on her own like that."

Dr Darcy hesitated. He studied Tom's face, the too-thin cheeks and serious eyes that carefully avoided his own. "She had only one daughter who was living in Australia and she died some years ago in a car crash. Mrs Maxwell flew out for the funeral but she's never been the same since. Her grandson, Thomas, wanted her to stay in Australia and live with him but she refused, point-blank. She's a stubborn woman, as you may have discovered. She will not allow any of her neighbours into the house. She pays no attention to any advice I give her. She's a solitary lady."

Tom nodded. "She hates people. Especially me."

"She's old and sad and lonely. She has no one to care for her so you must make allowances for that. Thomas is a kind grandson but his life is in Australia. He sends money each month which is entered into his grandmother's bank account. As far as I know, she never touches it."

"This...em...man...Thomas. What does he do?"

"He works for a television company. He makes travel documentaries. I believe he's quite good."

"Does he travel a lot?"

"I imagine he must. And now, I'd better make that phone call."

He moved past Tom and reached for the telephone, speaking urgently into it and asking for an ambulance to come immediately.

When he replaced the receiver, Tom was still standing in the same position. "All that travelling...his kids must hate it."

"I don't know, Tom." The doctor placed his hand on the young boy's arm. "Mrs Maxwell has never told me anything about his private life."

"Oh! Just wondered." Tom shrugged. "I mean it must be awful for them to have a father who's never there because he's travelling all over the world making documentaries. I'd hate that."

"I think we'd better go back inside and see how our patient is doing," said Dr Darcy. His voice was low and calm. He pretended not to notice the stiffness in Tom's body, the gulping way he swallowed as if there was no saliva left in his mouth.

Within a short time, an ambulance arrived. Mrs Maxwell tried to protest, gripping Tom with ice-cold hands and glaring at the ambulance men. "Go away. Stupid men. My grandson will take care of me." But her voice was only a croak and soon she was being carried from the house on a stretcher.

"Come with me, Thomas?" she begged. "Don't let them take me away."

"I'll go with her." Tom prepared to climb into the ambulance.

"That's not a good idea, Tom." Dr Darcy sounded firm. "Mrs Maxwell is confused. She needs professional help. Encouraging her in her delusions will not help either of you. Don't worry about her. She'll be in capable hands."

The blue light flashed but the siren did not sound as the ambulance left Elmtree Close. There were no traffic or people to slow its progress. Only Tom, standing beside the open gate of his great-grandmother's house, watched its departure.

Chapter Eight

I hate Beachwood Comprehensive! Keith Fowler has threatened to push my head down the loo if I don't hand over my lunch money. Liam Egan put a dog turd into my lunch box today. I'd love to rub his face in it. Mum doesn't know about the bullying. I can't tell her. She'll insist on ringing the school and that'll only make things worse for me. I want to go back to London. We had a row last night. She says I'm surly and bad-tempered. She only pretends to want to know how I feel. If I say the slightest thing about Beachwood, she gets uptight and goes on about me having to make more of an effort to be friendly and get to know people. It's not fair. She just suits herself and I have no rights whatsoever! She's drinking pints! Last night she went on a Reclaim the Night protest march. I'm half-way through my environmental project. Barry's photographs arrived this morning. Brilliant colour ones of birds that will soon become extinct if they don't stop cutting down the rain forests. They have feathers like rainbows. I wish Lester would write!

"Hey Parky! Over here." Keith was actually smiling. "Push over and make room for Parky," he ordered Liam.

"It's OK, I'll find my own table." Tom turned away from them. It was noon on Monday and the last week before mid-term.

"He wants to sit with the Virgos," sniggered Liam.

"Lay off him." Keith tapped his friend on the top of his head with the canteen tray then flung it on the floor. "Don't be like that, Parky," he said. "I was only joking about the lunch money. Let's shake. You're not such a bad guy."

Following their leader's example, the other boys offered Tom their hands. Duane Ryder brought over another chair and gestured towards it, inviting Tom to sit down. Tom was rigid with suspicion.

"Sit down," ordered Keith. The tough-guy image had disappeared and he was actually smiling. "We know it's been rough, you being new to the place and all. If you want to join our gang, you're in."

The other boys grinned at him. Cautiously, Tom sat down. The chair did not collapse. A whoopy bag did not splutter underneath him. Instead, Liam offered him a packet of crisps and Oliver gave him a Mars Bar. Tom was astonished. They were treating him like royalty, and all because Keith Fowler had offered him his hand in friendship.

Oliver nudged Keith. "Are you going to ask Tom to your party on Hallowe'en?" he asked.

Keith's mouth was full of flaky pastry, but he obediently gulped, rolled his eyes with the effort of swallowing and sprayed the table with crumbs. "I'm having a party in my place on Hallowe'en. It's the same night as that barn dance thing the sixth years are running. My parents are going so we'll have the place to ourselves. Do you want to come?"

The sixth-year students had organised The Beachwood Comprehensive Barn Dance in aid of famine relief. It was being held in the Swansbury Hotel and the pupils had been asked to each sell four tickets. Tom's mother had bought his four tickets and was bringing Conor and his parents.

"It'll be a gas. We're asking girls to come along as well." Keith guffawed. "But say nothing about it or there'll be loads of gatecrashers trying to get in."

Tom wanted to refuse. He did not trust Keith and his friends. But the need to be liked, to be accepted into a group, made him nod his head. Throughout the week, they included him in their activities. Tom had forgotten that life could be so easy. The taunting stopped. He could walk freely along the corridor without fear of being slammed against a wall. It was as if a great weight had been lifted from his chest. He began to smile, to make jokes, to feel human again. He was one of the crowd. They called for him on Friday night to go to the disco at the Beachwood Community Centre. He danced a slow dance with Jennifer and tingled all over when she sank her face into his neck. No one jeered them or put on a Cockney accent.

"Are you going to Keith's party on Wednesday?" he asked.

"Go to a party with those airheads? You must be joking!" She breathed against his cheek. He felt as if he was being tickled by a very soft feather. "They hang around with a much older gang and Keith is always trying to show them that he's really cool."

"But they said..." Tom's voice trailed away. "I was sure they said you were going."

When the dance was over he asked Keith why he had not invited Jennifer Hilliard.

"She's just a kid. A Jason Donovan teeny bopper. We're inviting *real* women." He winked meaningfully. "It'll be deadly. Just wait and see."

On Wednesday afternoon the phone rang.

"The gang's meeting in Fountain Square. Be there!" said Keith.

"I can't. I want to work on my project for that competition they're running on the environment."

Keith yawned. "It sounds like a real bore. You're one of the gang now, Tom. We go everywhere together. If you want to drop out just say the word. Maybe you've better things to do?"

"No, it's not that," said Tom, hurriedly.

"Good! Then we'll see you at the square."

Fountain Square was in the middle of Hobourne Park, a popular place for the teenagers of Beachwood to meet. But the fountain was dry and scummy brown leaves were slippery beneath Tom's feet. As soon as he saw the faces of his new friends, he knew that something was wrong.

"It's too cold to hang around here. Let's walk," said Keith. They moved away from the open area of the park and entered Twist and Shake. This tree-lined labyrinth of twisting trails was reputed to be haunted. Tom had walked through it once with Caro who had told him in the most blood-curdling tones that he might see the headless body of a ghost called Norton Hobourne at any moment.

"Did you ever see him?" Tom had asked and Caro had

looked dreadfully embarrassed.

"Not exactly." She had told him another long rambling story about her slumber party, an event that seemed to have included every activity except slumber.

Twist and Shake was narrow and dark. It had a musty smell of rotting undergrowth. Creepers hung from the limp branches like banshee hair. Very few people walked through this area of the park. Keith kicked the leaves under his feet and scowled.

"Big trouble," he said. "The party's off."

"Why?" Tom gasped, hiding his relief.

"My mother says so. She's always spoiling things for me at the last moment." He fingered his chin, peeling off the top of a pimple. "Everything's arranged. Grub and all that stuff. Everyone's going to go mad."

"They'll just have to understand," said Tom. "It's not your fault."

"Try telling that to them. They'll make my life hell, they will. If I'd told them sooner, they could have made other arrangements."

"I wouldn't like to be in your shoes, that's for sure," agreed Oliver Kerr.

"Is there anywhere else you could hold it?" suggested Tom.

Immediately the four boys looked at him.

"Like where?" asked Duane, quickly.

Tom shrugged. "I don't know."

"What about your place?" suggested Keith.

"My place!" Tom gasped. "No way. My mother would never allow it."

"But she doesn't have to know," said Keith. The boys moved in closer to him. "She's going to the barn dance."

"That's a brilliant idea, Tom," said Oliver. "Your place

is out of the way. No one'll know there's a party going on."

"No...no!" Tom could feel the ground shifting beneath him. "She'd never give permission at this late stage."

"Don't be such a wet, Parky! She doesn't have to know! We'll be gone before she gets back." Keith seemed to be trying to explain something simple to a very silly child.

Tom tried to move away from him but Keith blocked his path. He shook his head, sorrowfully. "We thought you were our friend, Tom. We thought you were one of us."

"But, I *am* your friend."

"Then prove it. It's only a small party. About eight of us altogether. That's not a lot, is it?"

Numbly, Tom shook his head.

Keith slapped him on the back. "Don't worry about anything. We'll bring everything, food and drink and—"

"Drink!" interrupted Tom, faintly.

"Just a few cans. You won't even have to supply the glasses. We'll be around about nine." He frowned. "You won't let us down, Tom. You're our *mite*! Wot are you, Tom?" This time the mimicry was teasing but it brought back the misery of Tom's first months in Beachwood.

"I'm your mate," he replied, and followed the boys as they headed back to Fountain Square.

Chapter Nine

I met Red Prescott on the way home. He's in fifth year and plays rugby with the Beachwood Blues. He says he's coming tonight and it's great about the pad. I wish I could go into a coma and not come out of it until tomorrow. Catalepsy should do it. Please God! Give me a twenty-four-hour catalepsy bug. Please! They're coming soon. Keith said only eight. That should be OK. Who'm I fooling? If Mum knew, she'd go spare. I hope she doesn't wear her Docs to the barn dance. I've enough problems!

Conor O'Carroll called and whistled appreciatively when he saw Tom's mother. He began to sing a song called "Lady in Red." Tom thought she looked about twenty-two years old in a slinky red dress without a back. At any other time, he would have felt embarrassed at the thought of his mother displaying so much flesh. But given the gear she'd been wearing since she came to Beachwood, it could be worse.

"Do you want a lift to Keith's house?" she asked him.

"No, I'll walk," Tom replied.

"Isn't it wonderful that Tom is making friends?" Helen beamed from her son to Conor.

"I told you there was nothing to worry about," said Conor in the tone of voice that suggested they had held long and serious discussions on this subject.

Tom smiled, feebly.

It was nine when Keith arrived in a hideous green devil mask, followed by what looked like an invading army. They swarmed over the house, settling into the kitchen, hall, lounge, breakfast room and the stairs.

Oliver checked out Tom's record collection and put on a Stone Roses LP, turning the volume up full. Some of the faces Tom recognised. Others were strangers who did not believe in making strange. They were mostly older boys and girls, carrying cans and six-packs. Everyone seemed to be talking at the top of their voices, gathering in large groups and ignoring Tom. Most of them did not seem to realise it was his house. When he tried to go upstairs to see what had caused a loud crashing noise from his mother's bedroom, the kissing couples who sat on the stairs told him to "back off" and he had to squeeze against the wall to get past them.

The crashing noise had been the breaking of the mirror on his mother's dressing table. Red Prescott and two of his friends had been playing rugby with a pillow. Red explained that the mirror had got in the way of his shoulder. He was flushed and exhilarated, tilting a Budweiser bottle to his lips. Tom was frantic. A couple lay on his mother's bed. They looked like statues. Lips glued together, they paid absolutely no attention to the rugby mayhem going on around them. When the promised food had not appeared, the starving hordes tackled the fridge and the freezer. Oliver and Liam, who were carrying on as if they were hosting the party, defrosted pizzas in the microwave. Tom felt like a stranded fish, opening and closing his mouth, saying, "No! You can't!" His words were lost in the growing hubbub.

"You've got to get them out!" he shouted at Keith.

"Great party, my man!" Keith shouted back. "Relax, enjoy it. Let loose, man!"

"Hi, I'm Lorraine Crowe. Is this your place?" A blonde girl with her hair in a French plait tapped his shoulder. He stared at her miserably and nodded. He could not remember having seen her at Beachwood Comprehensive.

"Does your mother know you're having this party?" she asked. Her eyes were large and grey. They glowed with sympathy and he could only shake his head. He was afraid that he would start to cry if he spoke. Earlier he had seen her with Danny Kane. Danny had tried to play his guitar but some older boys threw slices of pizza at him and told him to "belt up." After a few minutes he had shrugged and put his guitar away. He came over to join Lorraine, putting his arm across her shoulders and grinning ruefully.

"Some party, Tom. I was told it was going to be a music session. But these morons are turning it into a wrecking session. What made you invite so many people?"

"I didn't...never...Keith said only eight were coming. What'll I do!"

When Danny heard what had happened his face darkened.

"You've been set up. Keith Fowler's mother is so house-proud she wouldn't let fresh air into her place—let alone that lot. Keith likes to curry favour with the older crowd. He was after your house all the time. Word's been going around the village all week that there was a party on in Mill Hill on Hallowe'en. I didn't realise..." He fell silent and looked around the room.

Empty bottles lay on the floor. A broken glass glinted beneath the table. Cigarette butts left scorch marks on the carpet. Food had been trampled underfoot. In the kitchen, the freezer door hung open and pizzas sizzled and burned under the grill. The music slowed down. Eric Clapton crooned "My Darling, You Look Wonderful Tonight." Someone turned off the lights. Tom was dimly aware of muffled giggles and sighs as couples danced slowly past him.

He cleared his throat and blinked. "What am I going to do?" He bent down to pick up an empty can and crushed it in his hands.

"Don't worry. I'll rope in a few of the others to help. They're not all prats like Keith and his mob. I'll talk to Red. I'll tell him you're in deep trouble. He'll get them out."

"The last time I saw him, he was playing rugby in my mother's bedroom."

"We'll help you to tidy up when they go." Lorraine tried to reassure him. "It won't take—" Her voice stopped when the light snapped on.

"Hey, turn it off!" Liam shouted. He lifted his head from a girl's shoulders and glared belligerently at the person who dared destroy the romantic mood that had settled over the crowd.

Tom moaned and sank to the floor. He buried his face in his knees and tried to blot out the sight of his mother standing, her hand frozen on the light switch, her face a mask of horror as she looked around. Conor stood beside her.

"It's Parky's mother!" Word spread like a dry forest fire. "Let's cut out of here!"

Helen's lips were white and puckered. She walked to the stereo and switched it off.

"Get out!" she said, addressing no one in particular. Her voice was barely audible but everyone heard and obeyed on the instant. The kissing couples on the stairs had already untangled and fled. The statue-like pair on the bed came to life and bolted down the stairs. Young people climbed over the back wall and hurried along the embankment path. They vaulted the front gate and ran down Mill Hill. Conor disappeared into the kitchen to turn off the grill. Smoke billowed out and set off the smoke alarm in the hall.

"We'd better get going." Danny was nervously hugging his guitar to his chest.

"No, we can't leave him," cried Lorraine. "None of this is his fault."

"Stand up!" Helen stood before her son. Tom had never seen her so angry. He thought she was going to hit him, and ducked his head as if he had already taken the blow. She had always treated him in an adult way and he, understanding from a very early age that she trusted him, had given her very few reasons to discipline him.

"It's not his fault," Lorraine repeated. "That crowd just came and took over."

"Would you mind leaving my house, both of you!" Helen's eyes blazed. "Let my son do his own explaining."

"Come on, we'd better split." Danny had his hand on her elbow. "Lorraine's right. They took advantage of Tom. He didn't know this was going to happen."

In the kitchen, Tom could hear the clink of dishes as Conor loaded the dishwasher. Helen pressed her hands to her forehead. "I don't know you any more, Tom. What on earth possessed you to do such a terrible thing?"

"You wouldn't understand."

"Don't use that tone of voice on me!"

He stared at a cigarette burn on the carpet.

"Have you nothing to say for yourself?" Helen demanded.

"How can I say something when you object to my tone of voice?"

"Don't be so cheeky! All I want is an explanation as to why you filled my house with hooligans."

"I thought it was supposed to be *our* house!"

"You have a funny way of showing respect for our house." She continued to massage her temples. The veins on her hands were taut. "I've such a headache! And you're the cause of it. I met that horrible Mrs Fowler at the barn dance. I assumed they would be at home supervising their son's party but they had figured I should be doing the same thing. I don't envy Keith Fowler when his mother arrives home. Then she told me that you've been bothering Mrs Maxwell. Why didn't you tell me you'd met that woman?"

"When are you here to listen to me?"

"That's not fair!"

"It wasn't fair to bring me to this kip. I hate it! I want to go back to London. You don't care about my feelings. You're just wrapped up in your own stupid plans."

"I don't want you going near Mrs Maxwell again!" Helen screamed. "Do you hear me? Do you?" She reached towards her son and grabbed his arms, shaking him fiercely. Then she burst into tears and released him.

"Take it easy, you two." Conor came out of the kitchen. He put one arm around Helen's shoulders but

Tom flinched away from his touch. "What's happened to the mother and son I met just a few months ago?" he asked.

"Why don't you butt out?" Tom shouted. "You're not my father! I've never had a father."

Suddenly, he was sobbing. He ran from the room and up the stairs. In his bedroom, he locked his door. He cried for a long time. Helen called his name but he made no reply. Eventually, when he was too exhausted to cry any longer, he fell into a fitful sleep. He dreamed about his father. But when he woke up in the morning, he could only remember a faceless image. Before he rose from his bed, even that had disappeared. When he came downstairs the house had been tidied. His mother rose late. There were deep shadows under her eyes.

"I'm sorry about everything," Tom said.

"Talk to me, Tom. Tell me what's wrong. Why have you changed so much?"

"I want to go back to London! I hate this place."

She sighed. "Please Tom...please don't say that. I can't bear the thought of going back."

"And I can't bear the thought of staying!"

There seemed to be nothing else to say. Tom ached for the easy companionship they had left behind in London. The familiar pattern of each day. The friends he could trust. But mostly he ached for a man whose face he could not even imagine.

Chapter Ten

It's awful walking through Beachwood Village. I feel that everyone's watching me. Keith and his gang hang around The Greasy Spoon. They're mad over the party. Keith says I deliberately ratted on him and he's been in big trouble with his mother. Mum's looking a bit defeated. She no longer talks about college and she's stopped wearing Docs. Actually, she hardly talks at all about anything. I met Dr Darcy today. He doesn't know when my great-grandmother (her of the thousand poisoned tongues) will be home. She's been shifted from Beaumont Hospital to a nursing home called Limestone House. I wonder where it is?

The nursing home had wide bay windows and steps leading to the front door.

"What relation are you?" asked the nurse.

"Her great-grandson."

"Then you must be Thomas. She talks about you all the time."

Mrs Maxwell sat in a wheelchair in a recreation room. A television set was on and some of the old people watched it. Others stared curiously at him. Mrs Maxwell's head nodded. Tom thought she was sleeping.

"A special visitor for you, my dear," said the nurse in a loud voice.

Mrs Maxwell lifted her head and blinked. "Thomas, what kept you?" she asked. Her voice sounded raspy, as if she did not use it very often.

"I came as soon as I could." He sat down beside her and forced himself to hold the shaking hand she offered him. Her face looked even more withered and grumpy. "Did you bring me chocolates?" she asked, pettishly. "You always bring me chocolates. Bold boy! Where are my chocolates?" She slapped his hand. Tom was afraid she would fall out of her wheelchair.

"I have them here, grandmother. Look. Dairy Milk."

She did not seem interested in opening them but hugged them greedily to her chest, glaring at the other people in the recreation room. No one paid any attention to her.

"As soon as my back is turned, they steal everything from me," she whispered. "I don't like it here. The nurses are so cheeky, whippersnapper girls, that's all they are, singing at the tops of their voices and making my poor head ache." Her voice droned on and on. Tom's feet tapped with impatience.

"Tell me about Australia," he asked. "Why didn't you stay there with me?"

She looked slyly at him. "We'll go together, Thomas. You'll take me, won't you? You'll forgive me." Her grip became strong as she pulled him close to her. "Say you'll forgive me." Her eyes closed and her head drooped again.

He leaned forward, wanting to take the old woman by her shoulders and shake her until she woke up and poured out the words that he wanted to hear. It was towards the end of his visit that she began to sob. Tom held his breath.

"I should have..." He could see her chest, rising and falling as if she had run an exhausting race. "The baby...the baby...that was bad...bad for you, Thomas. I never told you. Your mother said it was for your own good and I agreed with her. That girl...oh, Thomas. I see her face all the time." She covered her eyes.

Tom could not stop trembling. "What about the letter the girl wrote?" he whispered.

"The letter. Burned letters, Thomas. Burned secrets and you never knew where she went. Your mother was right to burn them. You were just a boy. How could you be a father?"

"I loved her." His voice cracked.

The withered face blurred before his eyes, melted into a wavering blob that spoke hesitant, frightened words from the past. "It was for your own good, Thomas. Remember, Thomas. Your own good. When you asked where the girl went, I told lies. All those years...to forget...I want to forget, Thomas. Forgive...forgive..." Her chin sank towards her chest. A wispy snore escaped through her nose.

"Are you all right?" The nurse stopped beside him.

"I'm all right." His hand banged against his knee.

"Don't look so worried. She keeps dozing off like that. But I think she's had enough excitement for one day. You'd better leave now and let her have a proper rest." The soft pad of the nurse's shoes faded. He rose stiffly and walked away. That evening he wrote a letter.

Dear Mr O'Meara,

My name is Tom Parkinson. You knew my mother, Helen, a long time ago. I am writing to tell you that your grandmother is very ill. She is in a nursing home and I think she is suffering from senile dementia. I don't think she will live very long. She has told me about you and she wants to see you before that happens. My mother sends her love. She speaks very fondly of you. If you cannot come to Ireland could you please reply to this letter and send a photograph of yourself. I will give it to your grandmother. I hope you don't mind me writing to you but I am very worried.

Yours sincerely

Afterwards he worked on his project with a fierce concentration. Helen rang to say she was staying late to study in the college library.

"Remember, Tom, no parties! Joke! Joke!" But it wasn't really funny. It was after eleven when she arrived home. He pretended to be asleep. Her hand brushed his face before she left the room. In the darkness, he slid his hand beneath his pillow and touched the first letter he had ever written to his father.

Chapter Eleven

Today I drew a chart on the stages of destruction in a rain forest. It's all-out warfare. Humans against nature. A tree that grew for one hundred years, its heart cut out in ten minutes with a chainsaw. Animals and birds, refugees, their homes wrecked. Firebombs dropped on them. Defoliants poisoning them. Their food source destroyed. Genocide. Ethnic cleansing. Murder. The rape of the rain forest. Will nature fight back? Will it suffocate us when we no longer have any oxygen to breathe? Will it melt the ice caps and drown our cities? It will serve us right if that happens. I think I have a good chance of winning. That'll make them notice me!

In the staff room of Beachwood Comprehensive, Mrs Belton told the other teachers that Tom Parkinson seemed to have two left feet and was unable to walk the length of the classroom without stumbling or falling. "In the beginning he seemed to make a great effort to settle down. But he's become very withdrawn. No participation any more."

Mr Twomey, Tom's maths teacher, agreed. "He can't stop fidgeting in class. He doesn't seem to have made any friends. Have you noticed that? Even Caro and Jennifer have been blown out." He looked around the staff room.

"I wonder if he's being bullied?" Mrs Belton threw the question out to the group of teachers who were involved with 2B and they agreed to keep a close eye on things. But Mr Brown thought they were making a fuss about nothing.

"Lads will be lads," he said. "There's too much emphasis nowadays on mollycoddling them. If the lads are giving him a bit of a rough time, you can bet your life there's a reason. Lads have their own code of conduct and they'll always pick on the weak one who can't cut the ice. You should have seen the fuss he made when I took him abseiling. He has to learn to stand on his own two feet. It'll toughen him up for later life."

"That's true," replied Mrs Belton in a sweetly agreeable voice. "Perhaps we should introduce a course on bullying into our school curriculum. It would give our pupils experience in football hooliganism and mugging and gang violence and finally they could graduate to man's favourite sport, all-out war!"

"Spare me from the ravings of frenzied feminists!" Mr Brown moaned and walked briskly towards his geography session in 2B.

"Pathetic little man," muttered Mrs Belton and wondered if the time had come to give Helen Parkinson a ring.

When Tom's project on the rain forests was discovered on the floor of the boys' toilets, torn in half and streaked where the paints and ink had run together, none of the pupils in 2B seemed to know anything about it. Tom lifted the limp sheets of paper from the floor. He had brought it into school the previous day and handed it over to Mr Brown. The geography teacher had been busy and waved him aside, impatiently.

"Just leave it on top of my desk," he said. "I'll look at it later when I have time."

Now it was reduced to a heap of soggy mulch.

In 2B, the pupils stayed silent when he challenged Keith and accused him of being responsible. Keith spread his hands, palms out in a puzzled gesture, and said that he was very offended. How could Tom Parkinson make such an accusation without offering one shred of evidence? Tom looked around the classroom. Pupils chatted together, ignoring him, not wanting to be involved in his private war. But there was a sharp edge to their conversation as if they were embarrassed by the tension between the two boys. Caro looked miserably out the window. Jennifer had tilted her chair and was rocking forwards and backwards, her eyes staring at the ceiling, her cheeks flushed. Liam was making monkey sounds, jumping up and down in an exaggerated bow-legged movement and scratching under his arms.

Caro longed to interfere. She noticed that Tom had lost weight and pitied the blank expression on his face as he held the sheets of soggy paper before him. Paint had dripped from them and stained his trousers. But Tom had warned her to stay out of his business and she knew the reaction she would get from Keith and his gang if she said anything. She looked around at the boys who were not involved and sensed their discomfort. "Cowards!" she thought, furiously. "They hate what's happening but they're afraid of the slagging they'll get if they stand up for Tom."

A humming sound seemed to be going through the top of Tom's head. The project slipped from his hands. He made a sound that was almost like a grunt of pain and smashed his fist into Keith Fowler's face. The bigger boy was so taken by surprise that he fell back against a desk. He steadied himself and lunged at Tom. The two boys wrestled in the narrow space between the desks, trying to throw each other to the floor. Girls screamed at them to stop. Liam Egan stretched out his foot and tripped Tom, who fell against one of the benches. Immediately Keith had his knee on Tom's chest and had grabbed a handful of his hair. Tom bucked and threw him off.

"You're disgusting!" Caro shouted at Keith. "You're just a big, stupid bully!"

"She's right!" Jennifer thumped her desk. "You've been giving him a hard time since he came to this school."

"The Virgos are standing up for him again." Liam smirked. "Save me, Jennifer. Hold my little hand, Caro. I'm falling!" He screamed in an affected, high voice.

"I want my mummy!" Oliver pretended to cry.

"Mr Brown's coming." Duane had been keeping guard at the door. Keith shoved Tom away from him and walked back to his seat. "I'll finish this later," he panted.

The faces surrounding Tom seemed to be coming closer, making it impossible for him to breathe. He let out a deep shuddering sigh and dashed from the classroom. Outside in the corridor, he leaned his arms against the wall and buried his face in them. When he heard Mr Brown call his name, he turned in the opposite direction and ran.

It was raining outside. A knifing north wind cut easily

through his school uniform. Within a few minutes, he was soaked and shivering. He grabbed his bike, his feet slipping from the pedals, and cycled furiously towards Mill Hill. The key ring fell when he took it from his pocket but he managed to find the key. To his surprise the radio was on in the kitchen and Pat Kenny was interviewing a politician about unemployment.

Tom ran up the stairs and into his bedroom. His mother was sitting on the edge of his bed. Her head was bent as her eyes quickly skimmed over the pages of his private diary. At the sound of the door opening, she looked up. A stricken expression crossed her face and she flung the diary from her as if it had suddenly burned her fingers.

"Tom! What are you doing home from school? And you're soaking wet!"

"You were reading my diary!" he loudly interrupted her. "How dare you?"

There was a rule between them that a diary was private property, as sacred as the Holy Grail, as private and safe as the most precious gold nuggets in Fort Knox. To see his mother break this trust was more than Tom could bear. It made him feel naked, knowing that his most intimate, most private thoughts and feelings had now become her property.

"You were spying on me," he shouted. "I'll never trust you again as long as I live. I hate you."

His outrage gave him an opportunity to unleash his anger and misery. He snatched the diary from the bed and began ripping out pages, tearing them into flitters and flinging them at her.

For a moment, Helen seemed too dazed to do anything except sit mutely in front of him. Her hands reached towards him then fell limply to her side. She picked up a torn page and stared unseeingly at it. When she looked at him again her eyes were moist. She rose from the bed and put her arms around him. For a moment he struggled, pushing her away, shouting, weeping with fury. Then his anger and his strength left him. He slumped against her.

"I know it must seem terrible to you, Tom. I never thought I would do such a thing but I was out of my mind with worry over you."

"I don't know what you were worried about," growled Tom. He would never forgive her, no matter what she said or how repentant she looked.

His mother took a deep breath. "I had a phone call from Mrs Belton. She said you were withdrawn and inattentive. That you did not seem interested in making friends. Then there was that awful party and those visits to Mrs Maxwell. I didn't know what to think. You've been acting so strangely lately that I...well...I thought...I needed to know you again and I didn't... I feel so awful!" She began to cough, a throat-scraping embarrassed sound. "Please believe me, Tom. I'd no intention of reading your diary. But I had no lectures this morning and when I checked your room to see if you'd left any clothes for washing and saw it sticking out from under your pillow and I knew you'd put all your private thoughts into it and..oh, what can I say?" She was beginning to recover her composure. "I thought if I found out what was wrong, it would help me to help you. You'll be a parent yourself some day and then you'll know all about it!" This was her stock answer to Tom when he believed that she had overstepped the bounds of parental morality. "Why didn't you tell me you were being bullied?"

He did not answer her.

"I wasn't born before the great flood, Tom. I do remember what it was like to be a teenager. And if I remember rightly, it can be a bit like clawing your way through nettles. I know how important it is to be popular." She began to talk about her own teenage years. Something similar had happened when she was thirteen and a group of girls in her class had suddenly turned against her. She did not understand why and they did not offer any reason. Instead they ignored her and fell silent when she entered a room. They giggled behind her back and passed notes to each other which she knew had been written about her. The bullying had lasted for six months and it had been the most miserable time of her life.

"I used to wake up in the morning and the dreadful feeling was there, ready to jump into my mind. I didn't want to get up. I dreaded every day. Being bullied made me feel ashamed of myself. Even in my own eyes it belittled me, as if in some way I deserved it. I must be awful if I was so unpopular. All those girls could not be wrong. I desperately wanted to be liked, to be what your lot call 'part of the cool set.' Do you understand any of this, Tom?"

He kept nodding his head, fascinated by this peek into the olden days. Things didn't seem to have changed very much. "What happened in the end?"

"Instead of feeling ashamed, I began to wonder why those girls were treating me like that. Why did they need to make someone feel small so that they could feel big? That question was my turning point, Tom. It seemed to wash my mind clean of all the gunge. I began to despise them instead of despising myself. And they knew it. They started trying to include me in their group. I didn't want to know. I didn't need them. I preferred my own company and in time I made new friends, good friends."

Tom moved restlessly around the kitchen. "I know what you're saying but it doesn't make things any easier." He felt exhausted and shivery. It had been a long morning. Yet he was relieved that things were finally out in the open.

"I'm going to speak to the school about this."

"No! No!" Tom panicked. He could just imagine the reaction of the boys if that happened.

"But I have to report it." She spoke firmly. "Bullying like that cannot be allowed to continue."

"I don't want you to do anything. If you interfere, I'll never forgive you. Never. I've got to sort it out myself!"

Chapter Twelve

Mrs Belton held up two sheets of ripped white cardboard. The Chain Saw Massacre—A History of the Destruction of the Rain Forests had been written in red block letters across the front. Underneath, there was a painting of a felled tree trunk, with torn edges and an exposed inside that looked like an open wound.

"Would anyone like to tell me how this project happened to move from Mr Brown's desk to the boys' toilets?" The form tutor addressed her silent pupils. "Would anyone like to tell me how three months' work could be reduced to this!"

There was no answer.

"As no one seems prepared to accept individual responsibility then you must accept collective blame. I know that Tom Parkinson has been bullied. I am not a fool. I recognise the signs even if I cannot see who is carrying it out. Starting from this afternoon, you are detained until 4.30. Detention will continue each Wednesday afternoon until the Christmas break."

"But it's our half-day, Miss. That's not fair," cried Liz O'Rourke.

Mrs Belton placed the sheets carefully on her desk and pointed towards them. "I don't imagine that Tom Parkinson thinks this is very fair. Would you, if it was your project and some bright spark had tried to flush it down the toilet?"

Oliver Kerr put up his hand. "The match, Miss! Ireland are playing. It's an International, Miss!"

Mrs Belton ignored him. "Detention starts today," she announced.

An anguished growl came from the boys.

"I've got a ticket for Lansdowne!" Andrew Lee, an Ireland fan who wore tri-colour underpants and carried an Irish flag on the handlebars of his mountain bike, was furious. He jumped to his feet. "I've been looking forward to the match for weeks, Miss. Why should I be blamed?"

"Why don't you address that question to the person who *is* to blame?" Mrs Belton was unmoved by his tortured expression.

Andrew looked hard at Keith Fowler and sat down again.

"As this discussion is not going any further, then I suggest we open our books. I have to leave you for five minutes to collect your essays from the staff room. Study page 34 until I return."

As soon as the door closed behind her, bedlam broke loose.

"It's all your fault." Andrew rounded on Keith and grabbed his jumper. "You stupid thickhead. I've invested a month's pocket money in that ticket!"

"Lay off." Keith pushed him away.

"Andrew's right. Why should we carry the can for

you?" The boy who asked the question slammed his English book across the back of Keith's head. "I want to see that match on telly."

"We all do," shouted Duane. "You didn't have to go that far." He ducked his head and refused to look at Keith, unnerved by the fact that he had spoken against him.

Mrs Belton returned to the classroom and ignored the simmering whispers. She waited, allowing the silence to settle again as she scanned the pages of a copybook.

"It was Duane Ryder, Miss!" Keith put up his hand. "He destroyed the project."

As if he had been stung on the chin by a wasp, Duane flung back his head and stared in disbelief at Keith. "That's not true," he spluttered. "It wasn't my idea."

Keith looked accusingly at him. "I tried to talk him out of it but he's had his knife in Tom Parkinson ever since he started here."

"Liar!" Duane looked desperately around him.

"I don't like ratting on him, Miss. But it's not fair that everyone else has to suffer for something he did." Keith sounded very regretful.

"I didn't do it!" Duane shouted.

Mrs Belton closed the copybook. "You've made a very serious accusation, Keith. Have you any evidence to back it up?"

"Look at his nails, Miss. They're covered in paint."

Duane shoved his hands into his pockets.

"If Keith is lying, then you have nothing to fear. Show me your nails, immediately." Mrs Belton approached him.

Duane's nails were smudged with dark-green stains. Red paint was on the cuffs of his shirt.

"It's all his fault. He suggested it." He pointed angrily

at Keith. "Oliver Kerr knows. He was with us."

Oliver swallowed. "I...I...don't know what he's talking about, Miss. I never heard Keith say anything like that."

"Liam! You tell her," Duane pleaded. "Tell her it wasn't my idea."

Liam stared at his desk. "I don't know anything. Leave me out of it," he muttered.

"What fine friends you have, Duane." Mrs Belton gazed scornfully at the four boys. "I think a visit to Mrs Reynolds's office is in order for the four of you. There are a few other things we'd like to discuss with you. The rest of you continue from page 34. I do not want one word to pass your lips until I return."

"What about detention, Miss?" Andrew Lee asked, anxiously.

"That is something I will decide later." She left the room, herding the four boys before her.

When Mrs Belton came back from the principal's office, she announced that detention was cancelled. The four boys were not with her. She stood in front of her desk and raised her hand to stem the relieved cheers. Her expression was grim.

"I am ashamed of every one of you who allowed this bullying to take place. Tom Parkinson was a new pupil. He had left his friends in London, left everything that was familiar to him. And how did you greet him? Answer me that! Those of you who stood by and let it happen may not be as guilty as those who did the bullying. But by your silence, your refusal to help, you must carry some share of the blame."

The pupils sat in silence. Some were embarrassed, others fidgeted and stole sideways glances at each other. Caro and Jennifer felt very self-righteous, removed from the scorn that Mrs Belton was heaping upon her pupils.

That afternoon, they called to Tom's house.

"Those airheads have been suspended until the end of term!" Jennifer announced. "Serves them right!"

Tom did not reply. They followed him into the kitchen.

"Aren't you delighted?" Caro demanded.

"I couldn't care less," he retorted. "I want to go back to London."

"I'd hate that, Tom," said Jennifer. She lifted two oranges from a fruit bowl and tossed them in the air.

"What do you care?" he demanded.

"Not a lot! But I might, if you give me a chance."

"Oh! What sort of chance?"

"I could help you to do your project again." She tossed an orange at him and he caught it.

"So could I," said Caro. "That's why we came by."

"But it's going to be judged in two weeks."

"Then the sooner we start the better." Jennifer replaced the orange and began to count the days on her fingers. "Mrs Belton has given us time off to work with you in the school library for a few hours each day. It'll be a doss." She looked severely at him. "So, you needn't bother thinking about going back to London until the project's finished. Understand!"

"But it's impossible." Tom tried to hold on to his misery. "I'll show you all that's left of it."

In his room, the girls stared in dismay at the left-overs. Cluttered heaps of papers and charts and foliage littered a table in his room.

"No problem!" said Jennifer.

"It's a cinch!" echoed Caro. "But we'll need reinforcements. Where's the phone, Tom?"

They were bossing him, shutting him up when he tried to protest, opening the door to their friends, Aoife Johnston and Emma Patton. His room was a hubbub of noise. They were taking over his project, examining Barry's remaining photographs of the rain forests, cooing over the monkeys and the rainbow-feathered birds, making yucking noises at the insects, ploughing through his notes and sounding very impressed when they discussed what they called his "vital statistics." It was time for him to take over and restore order. Obediently, they listened as he gave each of them a certain task.

"Bossy boots," said Jennifer and narrowed her eyes in a way that he thought was very sexy.

Emma and Caro were in charge of statistics. They giggled so much that they were ordered into another room where, instead of working out figures, they painted rows of magnificent trees with pathetic faces and tearful eyes surrounded by stick men with menacing faces and chain saws. Tom was not sure that such illustrations suited the seriousness of his subject. But Jennifer persuaded him that people would relate more to the human-faced trees than they would to boring lists of statistics. The following evening, Danny, Red Prescott and Andrew Lee arrived, offering to help.

Work on the rain forest project was frenzied. Helen helped by making pots of soup and mugs of coffee. She was on her Christmas holidays and, in Beachwood Comprehensive, the holidays would be starting in ten days. The school was strung with tinsel and glitter. An enormous crib was erected at the flagstoned entrance. Choirs practised Christmas carols and end-of-term concert hysteria was well underway. On the last day before the competition, the young people stayed in Tom's house and worked through the night. When Helen woke next morning, she peeped into her son's room. Bodies, wrapped in sleeping bags, lay on the floor. Jennifer's head rested in a pile of dried leaves. Tom was slumped against the wall, an enormous colourful chart spread before his sleeping eyes. The Chain Saw Massacre was complete.

Chapter Thirteen

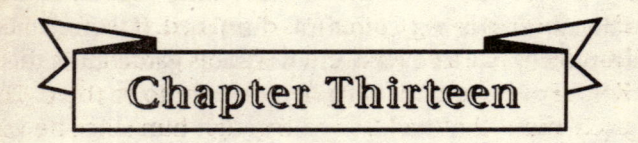

I did it. I won. When it was announced, everyone cheered. Red Prescott lifted me up on his shoulders and carried me around the school. Jennifer kissed me. Actually, it was only a kiss on the cheek but I have high hopes of working my way around to her mouth at the end-of-term disco tonight. Mrs Roberts, the librarian in Beachwood Library, presented the prize. A trophy and £50. Deadly! She's going to display my project in the library for two weeks in the New Year. It's hard to believe that things were so awful. Mum bought me a new diary. With a lock! Keith and his gang have faded out of the scene and Duane is not speaking to any of them. Watch my heart bleed. It'll be a long time before they bully anyone else. Jennifer Hilliard has really sexy eyes.

Tom heard the voices in the wooden shed as soon as he arrived home from school. He placed his Beachwood Environmental Trophy on top of the television and pulled aside the dining room curtains. They must have broken open the lock. His mother was in town buying Christmas presents and would be arriving home on the five o'clock train. He was on his own in the house. The thought of ringing Conor was dismissed. It would make him seem like a coward and it was his garden, his shed. Keith Fowler and his gang had no right to be there. The excitement that had flowed through him since he was presented with the award was wiped from his mind. Why couldn't they leave him alone?

"Hey Parky! We need some fresh air in here!" Keith shouted at the top of his voice.

His words were followed by the taunting sound of breaking glass as a stone came crashing out through the shed window.

"Parky, it's cold in here." Liam Egan stood at the shed door, holding a box of matches and a sheet of rolled paper in his hand. Oliver struck a match but the wind blew out the flame. Keith cupped his hands around another match and when the paper was ablaze, the boys disappeared back inside with it.

Tom could not believe what was happening. He rushed from the house and out into the garden. Smoke was beginning to billow from the broken window. When he reached the fire, he realised that it was small. Tightly-twisted rolls of paper blazed merrily but briefly then died into black ash on the stone floor. The boys had used it as a decoy to draw him out of his house.

They were waiting for him. Keith and Liam grabbed him. As he was dragged into the shed, he yelled and kicked out at Liam who was standing in range. Liam dodged him, breathing heavily. "Shut your face or I'll knock your teeth out," he hissed. His thumb jabbed against Tom's nose and sweaty fingers pressed hard over his lips. His arms were pinned behind his back.

"You've been nothing but big trouble ever since you came here, Brit." Keith punched him low on his stomach. Tom lurched forward. They were trying to force him to his knees. "You ratted on us over your stupid project and we're going to make you pay!"

Oliver giggled nervously and held a rope that they had found hanging on a hook in the shed. "Even your mumsy won't recognise you when we're finished with you."

Keith laughed. "Take it easy, lads. There's plenty of time. We won't drop him off the embankment until the train is going past."

"We're going to tie you up like a Christmas present and drop you over *real* slow." Liam's voice was soft. "We'll edge you closer and closer and then, when we see the train coming, we'll let you go."

They're only bluffing, Tom thought, trying to stay calm. But in his mind he could see nothing else but the long drop down the embankment and the vibrating beat on the tracks below as the train thundered past. Keith pulled his hair with such force that his head jerked back. Suddenly his top lip was free from Liam's fingers and he bit hard on the fleshy hand with all the fury of a cornered animal. Liam screamed and pulled his hand away, nursing it under his armpit. In the same instant, a coiled piece of paper that had fallen away from the heaped embers and had been slowly smouldering, burst into flame beside Keith's foot. The sudden gush of light in the darkening shed startled him. He stamped on it in panic before it scorched the bottom of his jeans. In doing so, his grip eased. Tom lashed backwards and the heavy heel of his shoe slammed into the bigger boy's shin.

While Keith grunted with pain, Tom used all his strength to break loose.

"Hold him! Get the rope around him!" Keith yelled at Oliver.

But Tom shoved him aside. He felt the ridge of rope under his feet for an instant then he was through the open doorway. He slammed the door behind him, sliding the bolt home. But Keith had already smashed away the jagged edges of broken glass on the window with the handle of a spade and was climbing through. He would catch Tom before he reached the house.

Tom changed direction and sprinted towards the garden wall. The embankment path would bring him past the field at the back of Conor's house. The boys were free and chasing him. Keith tried to grab his legs and failed as Tom reached the top of the wall and dropped out of sight. Liam and Oliver followed. Oliver had already thrown the rope over the wall and it lay like a waiting snake on the embankment path. Keith had mounted the wall further along and was poised, ready to drop on Tom if he tried to sprint past him. There was only one way to go. Tom ran forward and ducked between the barbed wire, frantically yanking the soft material of his school trousers free when it caught in the barbs. Then he was holding onto clumps of grass, his feet searching out footholds, slipping, sliding, his arm sockets being wrenched from the effort of holding his grip. With a loud curse, Keith jumped from the wall and stood with his friends at the edge of the embankment.

"Hey, Parky. We were only messing. Come back up. That's dangerous." Keith sounded frightened.

"You're not allowed down there," shouted Liam. His

voice echoed with the same fear. "A man fell from there and was killed last year."

Tom kept climbing. His chest wheezed. His mouth felt hot and dry.

"He's going to fall! I can't watch this." Oliver panicked, rounding on Keith and shouting, "It's all your fault, Fowler. You and your big mouth. Why couldn't you leave him alone?"

"Shut up! I didn't hear you saying you'd stay at home." Keith cupped his hands like a megaphone. "Listen, Parky. We were just trying to spook you. Let's call it quits. Climb back up and we'll shake."

"Get stuffed!" Tom panted and kept climbing.

"We'll throw down the rope and pull you up," Keith promised.

Tom had no energy left to reply. He was half-way down when he heard the train. His feet pressed firmly into a crevice, cold hands grasped a protruding flinty slab. He closed his eyes. The train roared, whistled shrilly and the noise filled his head, drowning out the dull snap of flint breaking under his fingers. The boys standing above and watching in terror did not hear Tom's scream as he fell, his body sliding and thumping and shuddering to the bottom of the embankment. They saw only the silent mime of a nightmare.

Oliver was crying, his mouth open as tears ran down his face. Liam dropped down on his hunkers and wrapped his arms around his head, rocking back and forth.

"I was only trying to spook him. Couldn't he take a joke?"

Keith panted, roughly trying to pull Liam to his feet.

Liam looked up at his friend. Slowly, as if he was moving through deep water, he stood upright. "We've killed him," he sobbed. "He's dead down there. Just like the man last year."

"We've got to bring him up." Oliver snuffled and wiped a trembling hand under his nose.

"Don't be daft! If you try to go down there, you'll fall as well." Keith swayed. His hand fell away from the barbed wire. "We've got to get out of here!" he whined. "We're going to be in big trouble if we don't."

"But we can't leave him," Oliver sobbed.

"Listen, do you want to go to jail for murder? That's what's going to happen if we're caught!"

"But it's not our fault. We had nothing to do with it," Liam cried.

"That's what I'm saying. No one knows we're here so they can't blame us. Come on! Let's go." He grabbed Liam's arm and pulled him roughly away from the edge.

"Get away from me! I'm going down. I don't care what happens." Liam could not stand still. He kept smacking his fist into his hand and shuffling from one foot to the other.

Keith began to walk away. "Are you coming?" He glanced pleadingly over his shoulder at the two boys.

They ignored him.

"It's not my fault! You'd better not put the blame on me," he shouted. Then, bending his head low, he sprinted along the narrow embankment path.

"We've got to get help. I'm going to find the phone in his house. Give me a leg up." Oliver tried to clamber over the wall.

"I'll wait with him until help arrives," Liam said.

He tied the rope securely to a barbed wire post and wrapped it between his legs, around his hip and opposite shoulder. It was the first time he had ever abseiled without a harness but he had no time to feel frightened as he walked backwards towards the edge of the railway embankment. Inky-grey clouds floated low in the sky. In the dying light, he passed the spot where Tom had fallen and averted his eyes but not before he had seen the sharp flinty edges of the break.

"Oh God! Make him alive, make him alive," he panted, running towards the still figure. His mind was noisy with the bullying words they had uttered so casually. Let's get him. Make him shake. Spook him out. Piss in his pants with fright. Follow the leader.

Why had he followed Keith Fowler? Echoed him? The hard man. The cool guy. Running like a frightened rabbit along the embankment path. He'd got his way all right. Tom Parkinson was well and truly spooked, his body curled around the withered tree and his hand resting on the edge of the track. Liam felt his stomach churn, hearing in his mind the thunderous roar of the train that had passed seconds before the boy hit the bottom of the embankment.

Tom was unconscious, breathing in shallow gasps, his face bloodied and grazed with gravel. As if sensing Liam's presence, his hand twitched and he uttered a low moan. Liam crouched beside him, touched him. Why had they chosen Tom Parkinson to bully? Where's your father, Parky? Is he a wart-face like you? Put the dog turd in his lunch box. That's always good for a laugh. Hey Parky, wot you got there? Wanna swop for a Mars Bar? Mega-laugh. Waylay him in the park for the big spit. Saliva all over his anorak. Bull's eye Fowler!

Why had they enjoyed the power it brought? Power that was stronger than the shamed voice in his mind that had so often said: "Enough! Leave him alone!"

Liam stretched out his hand and wiped a smear of blood from the side of the boy's nose.

"Oh Parky," he whispered. "Why did we do it to you?"

As the lights of rescue appeared along the top of the embankment path, Liam could not think of a single reason.

Epilogue

I don't know when I'm getting out of hospital. The specialist says I should sell my body to Lego and see if they can manage to put it together again. Very funny! I can't wait to go home. A broken arm, fractured skull, cracked ribs and Mum says I'll never be good-looking again. She would! Jennifer came in six times! Loads of people have been in. Nurse Desmond says my visitors are the noisiest in the whole hospital and that I'm supposed to be spending my time in bed recovering from a desire to fly—not holding all-day and all-night parties. Danny Kane, Red Prescott and Andrew Lee bought me a book called The Enchanted Canopy *between them. It's brilliant. All of Dancing on Grey Ash signed my arm cast. Keith Fowler has been expelled from school. Tough! Liam and Oliver were allowed to stay on but they were in big trouble and everyone gave them a really hard time. They came in and apologised. They looked as sick as parrots. It was all a big joke, they said. Spook Parky funtime. Ha, ha, ha! Liam is going to teach me to abseil on a rope when I get out. I don't remember the fall. But sometimes I dream about the train and the noise wakes me up. Nurse Desmond is really nice to me when that happens. She says the nightmares will stop after a while. Mum is beginning to look young again and tonight she was back in her Docs. She never stopped talking. She says her nerves are in shreds over me. Liar. It's because Dr Darcy told her old Mrs Maxwell is sinking fast. That means she's dying. That means funerals. And funerals mean that families come home from abroad. I should know! Sometimes they don't go away again.*

Conor looked sad tonight. I wonder what he's thinking. I like him a lot. Why does life have to be so complicated? I wonder if he got my letter yet. What if he comes? I'd die. But he won't. Why should he? Australia is very far away. It's the other side of the world. The upside-down part, actually. He won't come. I know he won't! I bet a million pounds I'm right!

Other Beachwood Titles

The Slumber Party

The Debs Ball

Summer at Fountain Square